D1193014

Saints and Scholars

TERRY EAGLETON

VERSO
London · New York

First published by Verso 1987

Verso
UK: 6 Meard Street, London W1V 3HR
USA: 29 West 35th Street, New York, NY 10001 2291

Verso is the imprint of New Left Books

British Library Cataloguing in Publication Data

Eagleton, Terry
Saints and scholars.
I. Title
823'.914 [F] PR6055.A/

ISBN 0-86091-180-2

US Library of Congress Cataloging in Publication Data

Eagleton, Terry, 1943—
Saints and scholars.

1. Wittgenstein, Ludwig, 1889-1951—Fiction.
2. Connolly, James, 1868-1916—Fiction. 3. Imaginary conversations. I. Title.
PR6055.A44S2 1987 823'.914 87-14991
ISBN 0-86091-180-2

Typeset by Leaper & Gard Ltd, Bristol, England
Printed by Biddles Ltd, Guildford, England

For
Herbert McCabe

This novel is not entirely fantasy. Nikolai Bakhtin, elder brother of the celebrated Russian critic Mikhail Bakhtin, was indeed a close friend of Ludwig Wittgenstein, the foremost English-language philosopher of the century. Wittgenstein did indeed live for a while in a cottage on the west coast of Ireland, although at a later time than suggested here. Most of the rest is invented.

One

At ten minutes to six on the morning of 12 May 1916, James Connolly was lying in a cell in Kilmainham gaol, Dublin, when the door opened and a small crowd of people trooped suddenly in. It is surprising how many officials are needed for an execution. Through the cell door filed, in this order, Sean McGrath and Damian Walsh, prison warders; Francis Xavier Mather, chief warder; William Martin, Governor of Kilmainham gaol; the reverend Thomas Kelly, curate of St Benedict's parish church, Dublin, and chaplain to the prison; Dr Kiernan O'Brien, chief medical officer of Kilmainham, and Henry Crichton, an English civil servant there to witness the proceedings on behalf of the Home Office. Present already in the cell were Robert Kearns and Patrick Doyle, warders assigned to guard the prisoner. McGrath, Walsh and Mather entered the cell first, to protect the more important officials behind them in case the prisoner should offer them violence. The nine men found themselves wedged shoulder to shoulder in the cramped space, jostling a little for standing room like fans on a football terrace.

Connolly was dressed in bright green overalls, which would help him to stand out against the red brick wall where he would be shot a few minutes later in the early morning drizzle. The overalls were made of thick canvas material, tight around the buttocks so that if he shat himself with fright it would neither stain too offensively nor spill out unpleasantly if he put up a struggle. He was holding a pair of blue rosary beads, though he did not seem to be praying. The beads would be removed from him in a moment in case he tried blasphemously to swallow them or strangle himself with them. A photograph of his wife, Lillie Reynolds, lay decently face downwards on the cell table, as though inspected and done with. All the warders carried heavy wooden truncheons beneath their uniforms, in case the prisoner resisted and needed to be stunned. McGrath and Walsh were also wearing revolvers in shoulder holsters beneath their jackets in case Connolly, despite having been strip-searched that morning, had somehow managed since then to fashion or procure a weapon whose use he was reserving until this moment. Both Kearns and Doyle carried with them a pair of handcuffs, normally hooked to their belts but now loose and ready in their pockets. Dr O'Brien had with him a large black bag containing a hypodermic syringe primed with a heavy sedative. The bag also contained some extra equipment, to avoid the indelicacy and possible incitement to panic of having this on show: a heavy mouth gag made of a thick square of brown leather with attached buckled thongs, and a straitjacket. If Connolly put up a fight the chief warder could decide between several means of restraint at his disposal: shooting, stunning, doping, gagging or straitjacketing.

Henry Crichton was thirty-eight years old, ten years younger than the condemned man. On the previous morning he had kissed goodbye to his wife on the doorstep of their detached house in Farnborough and had taken the train to Liverpool, where he had caught the ferry to Dublin. He had never visited Ireland before; he worked in a department of the Home Office which dealt with prisons, not with Irish affairs. He had had an uncomfortable voyage, most of it spent vomiting in one of the boat's lavatories. He felt embarrassed by his sickness, and contrasted this with the apparent unconcern of his fellow vomiters. Some of them spent their time passing regularly to and from lavatory to bar, downing and upping stout as the boat flopped and staggered, sometimes vomiting and urinating simultaneously and exchanging comradely curses with one another. It occurred to Crichton that his stomach had already felt a little off on the train to Liverpool, perhaps in anticipation of the event he was about to witness over the water. He had no idea why he had been selected for this assignment, or what he was supposed to do when he got there. He had met only three or four Irish people in his life, and had never even seen anyone seriously ill. He wondered vaguely whether he had been chosen out of malice on the part of a superior. He was self-conscious about his boyish, guileless appearance and suspected that someone higher up in the Home Office had decided it might season him a little to watch someone get shot. There were a lot of ex-military types among the senior administrators who groused ritually about the effeminacy of office work.

Standing in the cell, Crichton was surprised at how small Connolly was. He had imagined him as a big man, perhaps unconsciously influenced by his reputation as a powerful speaker and militant labour activist. He did not know that Connolly had been brought up in an Edinburgh slum, in conditions unlikely to breed a flourishing physique. He noticed that the prisoner looked haggard and sick-faced, which he understandably ascribed to fear. It did not occur to him that Connolly looked this way not mainly because he was afraid, though he was, but because beneath his green overalls he was heavily bandaged as a result of the wounds he had received in the Dublin street fighting. His left ankle had been badly shattered by a sniper's bullet, which was why he was lying on the cell bed rather than, as custom demanded, sitting at the table. It was conventional procedure for a condemned man to receive his visitors sitting rather than lying down. William Martin, the prison governor, was uneasy at this swerve from tradition: for Connolly to receive the execution party lying down seemed faintly insolent, like guests arriving at a party to discover their host in bed. He had instructed Kearns and Doyle to try propping the prisoner up at the table, hooking his feet around its legs to lend him ballast, but Connolly had keeled over immediately and was only just prevented from crashing on to the stone floor. Until three hours earlier that morning the prisoner had not even seen the inside of the death cell; he had been lying in a bed in Dublin Castle hospital where for the past few days the doctors had been working hard to assemble him into one piece ready for execution. He had already received a considerably higher dosage of drugs than the medical team would have dreamt of using on an ordinary patient. There was a fear at one point that his foot might have to be amputated, a small piece of him that might cheat the firing squad. When Crichton was told of this he had been reminded of the joke about the old lag who requested that several limbs he had had amputated in prison should be mailed as mementoes to his old mother, and who was finally accused by the prison officers of trying to escape. William Martin did not want to risk the sentimental mythology consequent on marching up to a sick man's bedside and carrying him off to be shot. The army had already had to endure the embarrassment of court-martialling Connolly propped up in bed, and wanted as little more unconventionality as possible. Connolly had to be brought to the wall and shot while there was still blood in him. Francis Mather, the chief warder, had dreamt in a nightmare that he was dragging the condemned man along in a race against time, while bits and pieces of Connolly were spilling out on to the floor and blowing away in the wind. Mather kept stooping down on the run, stuffing the pieces back into the prisoner, but Connolly was getting emptier with each step and by the time they emerged into the prison yard he was flapping like an empty mail sack. Only one bit of him was left, a twitching bulge in the sack where his heart was, and Mather kept his hand firmly over this and nailed the sack quickly to the wall, hoping that the bulge would provide an adequate target for the rifles.

Crichton saw that the prisoner had a small row of books propped on his table between two empty tea mugs, a bible or perhaps prayer book, a sheaf of dog-eared pamphlets and a few bulky hardbacks. He knew that Connolly was a writer and wondered whether he had spent his last days perusing his own works. He did not look to Crichton like a literary man. At the moment he looked more like a stunted navvy on a Sunday outing, for despite the overalls his face and head had a curiously scrubbed, scraped look, the black hair cropped close like a skullcap and the Groucho Marx moustache trimmed sharply back.

The men in the cell fanned out into two rough ranks and looked down at the prisoner as if waiting for him to rise in greeting. It was customary for the chief warder to address the condemned man first, as the only official present sufficiently menial to know him personally but sufficiently high in rank to take an initiative. Mather rested his eyes on the outstretched Connolly and said, 'All right, Jim ...', somewhere between an order and an enquiry after his health. Connolly looked back at Mather and said, 'All right'. If he had spoken at more length they might have noticed that his accent was Northern Irish with a faint tinge of Scottish.

Crichton was wondering how they were going to get Connolly out of the cell. He did not know that condemned convicts were not expected to rise and walk to their deaths, even if they were capable of doing so. If Connolly had been sitting in a chair in accordance with regular practice, either Walsh or McGrath would have kicked the chair away suddenly with their foot on a signal from Mather, and while the prisoner's arms were outstretched to break his fall the other warder would have seized and handcuffed them. This was established death cell routine, though it was a tricky operation and easily bungled. Warders, however experienced, were likely to be nervous at the time, and had to rehearse the manoeuvre several times before the morning of execution, using each other as guinea pigs. Practically speaking it was not really necessary to kick away the prisoner's chair, but from a psychological viewpoint it was a useful piece of ritual violence which broke the ice for the larger piece to come. It was a symbolic announcement that the rough stuff had begun, which converted the prisoner at a stroke into an object and so made it easier for warders who by now knew him well to carry him to his death. It assumed that he would not come quietly, thus defining him as potentially violent, cowardly and uncooperative. There would be something indecorous, even nauseating, about executing a man who rises casually from his chair when you enter and walks with you voluntarily out of the door. One would risk the intolerable possibility of his passing a few remarks about the weather, or enquiring after your children.

In this case, since the prisoner was not seated, Walsh and McGrath moved across to his bed, draped his arms around their shoulders and helped him gingerly to the floor. Crichton noticed that Connolly heaved himself upright a little as they approached, to make this easier. Crichton moved instinctively out of the way of the cell door, clearing a path for the prisoner to be carried through. He was not aware that condemned convicts do not exit from their cells through the door by which they came in. It would be needlessly troublesome to march someone about to be executed down a maze of corridors, especially if he was screaming or defecating and needed to be dragged. It would also be imprudent to allow other condemned prisoners to witness all this at close quarters, perhaps hearing their colleague being borne shrieking past their door. While McGrath and Walsh held Connolly upright, Kearns and Doyle moved aside a small wardrobe which stood against the wall of the cell opposite the bed. The wardrobe shifted easily, unencumbered with fur coats or evening dress. There was another door concealed behind it, which Mather unlocked with a key. He stepped through the door himself, and beckoned the warders to bring Connolly through. Father Kelly went in after him, and the other officials followed behind. Crichton found himself in a bare concrete shed rather like an empty garage.

Immediately inside the door a stretcher was lying on the ground, and Walsh and McGrath lowered Connolly on to it. Then they picked the stretcher up at either end, and the party moved a few paces across the narrow shed to another door opposite. Crichton did not realize that he was in the execution chamber, of which Connolly's death cell was merely a walled-off section. A condemned prisoner, unknown to himself, spends his last days almost within spitting distance of the gallows. The gallows, which some in Westminster thought a more suitable end for Connolly than a bullet, was at the far end of the room to the left, but Crichton did not register this because he imagined a gallows as looking something like a guillotine, a wooden structure with steps mounting to a platform. Since it would be awkward to get a frenzied man up a flight of steps, the gallows was in fact a simple trapdoor in the floor of the shed, which was why Crichton did not notice it. There was a low concrete beam above it, from which the noose would be suspended. Father Kelly was bending over Connolly's stretcher murmuring to him, his finger crooked as a bookmark in his missal. He had heard the prisoner's last confession a few hours before, and had given him communion. Mather opened the door on the far side of the shed, which was unlocked, and the execution party emerged into the dim morning light.

They were in the prison yard. To their left was the dull brick wall against which Connolly would be shot, heavily chipped with the bullets of previous executions. To their right, eight soldiers of the second battalion of the Lancashire Fusiliers, the regiment's yellow plumes stuck in their caps, stood rigidly to attention beneath a fine rain. One of their rifles was loaded with blank ammunition. The eight men had been specially chosen for marksmanship, good character, steady nerves and discretion. They had been put through several rehearsals of this moment with lifelike dummies for targets, and would be granted certain privileges in compensation for the distressing nature of their task. A few men in civilian clothing hung around unobtrusively on the far side of the yard, members of the British intelligence service. Out of the firing squad's vision, a warder who had been waiting in the yard approached with a green canvas bag, nattily matching the prisoner's overalls. McGrath, Walsh, Kearns and Doyle raised Connolly to his feet, while Kearns handcuffed him behind and the new warder placed the green bag over his head. This was to spare him the sight of the firing squad, which he had already seen clearly enough, but also to spare the firing squad the sight of him. Father Kelly continued to murmur to Connolly through his hood, fidgeting nervously with his missal.

At this point the proceedings, smooth so far, hit a slight snag. It became obvious to Walsh and Doyle, who were holding the prisoner upright, that he would not be able to stand by himself to be shot. Walsh communicated this discovery to Mather in a low tone, who considered it briefly. It was no good lying Connolly against the wall on the ground, since he would present too meagre a target. Nobody on the other hand was particularly keen on holding upright a man about to receive a volley of bullets. Mather stepped across to the governor and made a suggestion in a rapid undertone. Martin nodded a little grudgingly, and walked over to confer with the lieutenant in charge of the firing squad. Martin then nodded to Mather, who sent Walsh back into the cell for the chair on which Connolly would have been sitting in the normal course of events. The lieutenant walked down the rank of soldiers informing them of a slight change of procedure. Walsh re-emerged from the gallows shed carrying a chair, and Connolly was seated on it against the wall. Had it not been for his hood he would have had a grandstand view of his own execution.

When the warders had got the condemned man upright on the chair and stepped back, Connolly began to tilt over sideways towards the ground and had to be hastily propped up again by hand. Mather had a word with McGrath, who disappeared into the gallows shed. He was away rather a long time. The Fusiliers were stood at ease by their officer and two of the warders continued to keep Connolly vertical in his chair, while Father Kelly hovered irresolutely around him. Finally McGrath reappeared carrying a length of rope. He and Walsh proceeded to tie Connolly to his chair, looping the rope over his chest and knotting it firmly behind. In his green hood and roped canvas overalls the prisoner now looked like a trussed dummy, the last vestiges of humanity fully erased. Father Kelly and the warders retired to one side of the soldiers, and the lieutenant, after a nervous glance in the direction of Governor Martin, gave the order to fire. Seven real bullets sped towards Connolly's chest, accompanied by one blank. The event was not historic, but would become so retrospectively. The men in the yard that morning could not know that in unmaking James Connolly they were helping to undo themselves.

History records that on 12 May 1916, James Connolly, Commandant-General of the insurgent republican forces of the Irish Volunteers and Irish Citizen Army, and vice-president of the provisional republican government of Ireland, was shot strapped to a chair in Kilmainham gaol. But history does not always get the facts in the most significant order, or arrange them in the most aesthetically pleasing pattern. Napoleon survived the battle of Waterloo, but it would have been symbolically appropriate if he had been killed there. Florence Nightingale lingered on until 1910, but this was an oversight on history's part. Byron should have gone down fighting in the war of Greek independence, not died of a fever in the midst of it. Seven bullets flew towards Connolly's chest, but they did not reach it, at least not here they didn't. Let us arrest those bullets in mid air, prise open a space in these close-packed events through which Jimmy may scamper, blast him out of the dreary continuum of history into a different place altogether.

Two

Late in the evening of James Connolly's non-execution, Bertrand Russell was drinking claret in his rooms in Trinity College, Cambridge, when there was an imperious tap at his closed outer door. Russell winced testily into his wine-glass: partly because one did not disturb a man who was sporting his oak, partly because he knew who was most likely to. Opening his oak a few grudging inches he saw a wiry man in open-necked shirt and heavily patched baggy grey trousers staring at him with an expression of outrage.

'Russell,' the man said, 'I'm going to kill myself.'

Russell nodded briefly and held the door a little further open in a perfunctory gesture of invitation. His visitor shook his head firmly.

'You must come to my rooms immediately.' His voice was high-pitched, querulous, Teutonic.

Russell sighed and went back into his room to scoop up the claret bottle and a glass. He knew there would be no drink in Wittgenstein's rooms, in fact that there would be nothing there whatsoever apart from a single wooden chair. Walking back to the door a thought struck him and he hurried back to pocket some cigarettes. Listening to Wittgenstein could be a lengthy business. He thought vaguely of snatching up a blanket from his bed, as Wittgenstein believed any form of heating in his room to be fatally weakening, but reflected that this might rashly indicate a readiness to stay long. Armed with these comforts he slammed his oak and accompanied Wittgenstein down the narrow staircase and out into the dim light of Great Court. Over to their right a group of undergraduates in evening dress, trousers rolled to knees and shirt-fronts crazily askew, were hoisting each other up into the fountain where Byron used to tether his pet bear. They struck saucy poses to each other as they splashed about, hairy oarsmen with pouting lips and coyly crooked knees. The two small dons plodded in silence past the porter's lodge and through Great Gate, crossed the cobbles of Trinity Street and entered the dank cavern of Whewell's Court where Wittgenstein had his rooms. Russell noticed to his irritation that his companion was humming a cheerful tune, vaguely Schubertian. A young man wearing spats and a knee-length frilly purple dressing gown came dashing out of Whewell's Court clutching two bottles of white wine by the neck and brayed suddenly to some companions across the street. Perhaps he was in fancy dress, thought Russell, though in Cambridge it was hard to tell. The two philosophers mounted the staircase in single file to Wittgenstein's rooms, and Russell picked up a deckchair from a stack of them outside the door. There was no furniture in the room, and no books: Wittgenstein read only detective stories and St Augustine. Skilled by now in manipulating deckchairs, Russell flipped his open with one deft hand, arranged his glass and bottle on the carpet and waited for his colleague to begin. Wittgenstein sat in the single chair, examined the ceiling closely, looked with sudden anger at Russell as though he had just broken wind, and placed his hand to his throat as though testing himself for strangulation. This was the room in which he conducted his celebrated seminars, sitting in silence for ten minutes or more while his eyes rolled and his body writhed in agony, labouring to give birth to an insight.

His colleagues would sit around watching him attentively, like the world press viewing the last threshings of a gas chamber victim or a group of doctors observing an acutely constipated patient.

'A man,' Wittgenstein announced suddenly, 'might have a stoat or other small animal in his clothing and be unaware of it.' He paused and glanced irritably at Russell. 'You agree this is possible?'

Russell considered briefly. 'It seems unlikely,' he concluded.

Wittgenstein made an impatient motion with his hand. 'Don't be so ridiculous, Russell, of course it's possible. Let's say that the man has left his trousers in a field, having taken them off for some purpose, and a stoat or other small creature, say a skunk or mongoose or hedgehog, crawls into them. Then the man puts on his trousers again and walks away ignorant of this fact.' He eyed Russell warily. 'You grant that this is entirely feasible?'

'Oh, come on,' Russell protested. 'How on earth could a man have a hedgehog down his trousers and not know about it?'

Wittgenstein stared at him intently for a moment. 'Very well,' he said finally, as if charitably conceding a point to his companion's slow-wittedness. 'Perhaps not a hedgehog. But a stoat certainly, you would agree with that?'

'Stoats are fairly hefty creatures, you know,' Russell observed cautiously. Had Wittgenstein been seized with a fear that he was infested with vermin?

Wittgenstein grasped the top of his head with both hands and wrenched it violently in the direction of the window. 'You are being obstructive, Russell,' he snapped. 'This evening your mind seems for some reason repugnantly literal and commonplace. Very well,' he sighed heavily, 'let's compromise on some *very* small creature, say a dormouse. A man could carry a dormouse in his trouser leg in complete ignorance of the fact.'

'All right,' said Russell for the sake of argument.

'And then perhaps somebody, let's say the man's wife, might notice this dormouse wriggling about and say to him, "What's that thing poking around in your trousers, Henry?", or George, or whatever the man's name happens to be?'

Russell suppressed a snigger. 'Yes, Wittgenstein, she might,' he agreed, composing his features quickly.

Wittgenstein eased back a little in his chair, the tip of his nose quivering slightly, a sure sign, Russell knew, that he was approaching conceptual orgasm. Otherwise his face was almost expressionless, set in a rigid mould but with a hint of suppressed craftiness about the lips, like a smuggler sauntering through customs.

'But the same man, Russell, couldn't have a pain in his foot and not know about it?'

Russell examined this too quickly. 'He might be under an anaesthetic,' he ventured.

Wittgenstein looked at him in disgust. 'A man under an anaesthetic,' he replied witheringly, 'isn't a man who is in pain but doesn't feel it, he's simply a man who is not in pain.'

Russell conceded his sloppiness with a curt nod.

'So it would be queer to say,' Wittgenstein continued, a small flourish of triumph taking root in his voice, 'that I know that I am in pain.'

Right now, thought Russell gloomily, it would certainly make sense for me.

'Since,' Wittgenstein went on, 'There's never any possibility of my *not* knowing that I'm in pain. Having a pain in my foot, in short, isn't the same as having a mongoose down my trousers.'

'I thought you said you were going to kill yourself,' Russell remarked.

Wittgenstein seemed not to hear. Rising from his chair he lay down carefully on the carpet, lowering himself gingerly as though depositing some frail goods of inestimable value, with the back of his head towards Russell and his feet pointing to the wall. Russell took advantage of his own temporary invisibility to swig from the bottle rather than bother with the glass, and commented to Wittgenstein's feet: 'I met Moore in Neville's Court before lunch. I think he's finally gone over the edge. He held up his hands in front of my face and said, 'How do I know these hands exist?' I told him to check if his arse was wiped. Silly bugger.'

Wittgenstein said nothing for a long time. Russell wondered if he had gone to sleep, then remembered he rarely did. Then the Austrian's voice, slightly muffled, announced from the floor: 'There is no possible context in which such a doubt could have meaning.' He cranked up his head slightly. 'As if a man were to buy several copies of a daily newspaper to check that what the first copy said was true.'

Russell, failing to grasp this remark, stared glumly out of the curtainless windows towards the dusky towers of Christ's College. The evening was not proceeding as festively as it might. When Wittgenstein called he had just returned from High Table, where the Master had fallen off his chair again. However firmly the Senior Combination Room butler wedged him in, he always managed somehow to slide out. They had tried chairs with high stout arms, apparently impregnable, and the butler had even taken to roping him unobtrusively to his seat with the arms of his gown, stained with a half-century's high living. Perhaps, Russell thought, they should get him a baby-chair and mash up his grouse with a spoon. During dessert in the Senior Combination Room he had begun his parrot imitations again, his loose leaking mouth waggishly puckered, piping and screeching down the dark mahogany table and holding up two withered claws to the grimly averted heads of the Fellows. 'More birdseed, please,' he shrilled to the butler, a burly young ex-Marine with carte blanche from the Domestic Bursar to sit hard on obstreperous Fellows during guest nights. But this writ stopped short of the Master, a Nobel prizewinning mathematician now quite incapable of recalling what subject he was in. The affair was the scandal of Cambridge; the Visitor had refused to act, cowed by the Master's aristocratic connections. The old man's sexual predilections were shamelessly overriding college democracy on the question of new Fellows: almost every Fellow down at the end of the table that evening had been blond, rangy and well under thirty. Wittgenstein himself never dined, objecting to the fact that the High Table was raised a symbolic six inches above ground level. For a while he was served at a small card table in the Hall, then gave it up altogether.

Wittgenstein rolled over onto his stomach, his face craning eagerly up at Russell from carpet level. Raising his right hand, he spread the middle and index fingers in the shape of a V and thrust them vigorously up and down.

'Russell,' he asked, 'What does this mean?'

Russell repressed his first response, remembering his colleague's notorious puritanism. 'That, Wittgenstein, is a crude gesture of contempt.'

Wittgenstein sat up suddenly and tucked his ankles beneath his thighs, regarding Russell with a secretive smile. The two men, facing each other in the dull light of the empty room, had a curious resemblance to fellow gnomes on a garden rockery. Russell, lolling in his deckchair, puckish and puppetlike in movement, gave the impression of being pointed all over, from his sharp chain and scrawny elbows to his dainty feet. His waist was improbably slender, nipped in like a ballerina's. Only the sudden beaked nose and fleshy lips qualified this appearance, protruding from his leanness like an elusive flash of some fatter, more carnal man within. His hair flew off his head at an acute angle as though he was permanently electrocuted, crimped and terraced, a jagged thrust of growth at odds with the ascetic face, as though he was wearing somebody else's hair absent-mindedly. When he grinned he looked like a demented pixie, but his shaggy head lent him an authority denied by the childlike, slightly dandified body. Wittgenstein was likewise lean and dapper in build, with brown eyes so piercing that he seemed chronically startled. With the lithe physique of a long-distance runner but the haughty bearing of a patrician, he shimmered with a compressed inward energy like a man on a short fuse about to explode, his irascibility as tangible as a bowler hat.

Wittgenstein tried the gesture thoughtfully a few more times, now moving only his hand, now jabbing flourishing V-signs to the ceiling with an upward thrust of the elbow. He seemed delighted by his discovery. He stood up and bent down in front of Russell from the waist, one finger pointing arbitrarily upwards.

'I saw a young man make that sign on King's Parade. He was running across the street and collided with a bicycle. He made the gesture to the cyclist, who returned it instantly, in what I would call an intuitive pact. And I thought to myself: that is *language*.' He paced meditatively back to his chair, his finger still raised as though he had forgotten where it was. 'That's why,' he added, staring with sudden surprise into his left cuff, 'I decided there and then to kill myself.'

Russell was thinking of the unusually pointed breasts of a young woman he had met at Ottoline Morrell's house a few evenings before. Perhaps she was remotely related to him; most people he met at Ottoline's seemed to be relations of some kind. They had danced together without music on the front lawn at midnight, and then Ottoline had swept up in her green turban with some gangly, consumptive-looking Midlands schoolmaster whom she was passing off as a literary genius and who was passing himself off as a coalminer. The girl had wandered meekly off with the gangly genius in the direction of the shrubbery. Perhaps he was humping her right now.

'What this reveals,' said Wittgenstein, shaping another V-sign, 'is the inner form of all language. What does this gesture *reflect*, Russell? Nothing. There's nothing *behind* it, it's merely what it is. I grasp its meaning, ultimately, by *doing* it.' He did it again. Then he leaned across to his colleague, lowering his voice confidentially. 'Don't you see the intolerable mystery of this? *Everything is exactly the way it is*. Everything is the way it is and not some other way.'

Russell allowed his thoughts to drift back from the sharp-breasted young woman. 'The trouble with you, Wittgenstein,' he murmured wearily, 'is that you've never managed to rid yourself of the illusion that philosophy has something to do with everyday life.'

'No!' shouted the Austrian in a strangulated voice, leaping to his feet. 'Philosophy has nothing to do with life!' He sank on his haunches before Russell's chair and clutched one of his ankles, his face dark and distraught. 'Give it up, Russell, give it up!' he commanded, like the pleading spouse of an alcoholic. 'Philosophy is merely what blinds us to the fact that everything is just the way it is. Everything is open to view, nothing is concealed. No grounds, no essences, no first principles. What philosophy can't grasp is an everyday gesture like this' — and he gave Russell's ankle a painful squeeze.

'If you've solved the riddle of life,' said Russell, coldly disengaging his ankle from Wittgenstein's bony grasp, 'Why are you so keen to kill yourself?'

'Perhaps because I don't like the answer. Because it

means there's nothing left for me to do. I've thought myself out of a career. Philosophy! The porter knows as much of it as I do. He doesn't know that he knows, but that's why he knows. A porter, Russell, is simple. What is it to be simple? Is a broom simple? Or is it complex, composed of a stick and brush?'

'You're philosophizing again,' said Russell, pouring himself some claret. 'You detest philosophy just like a philosopher. You speak like an old roué weary of copulation.'

'The metaphysical itch, Russell,' Wittgenstein whispered. 'The will to knowledge. It's a sickness. The rotten apple of Eden. I know absolutely nothing. I know that what happens, happens. At eight o'clock each morning my bedmaker enters this room, sweeps the carpet and leaves again. But that isn't enough for philosophy. We have to pick and scratch, unlock the essence of carpets and the inner structure of the act of sweeping. My bedmaker sees through such an absurdity without knowing it. The people have never sought knowledge. They simply do what they do, live in the innocent self-evidence of their gestures.' He raised his leg suddenly in the air and wiggled his foot. 'How does philosophy take the measure of *that*?'

'It isn't supposed to,' replied Russell irritably. He could feel the impulse to argue coming on, and resented this weakness. He would only despise himself later, like a reformed overeater wheedled into a pork pie. 'You can't stop believing that philosophy must have something to do with life, and then feel depressed when it doesn't. Like someone who kills himself because he can't play a tune on a carrot. Yesterday I was taking a cab ride in London to visit Leonard Woolf and the cab driver recognized me. He had the common man's image of a philosopher. He said to me' — here Russell did a passable imitation of a cockney accent — '"What's it all about then, gov?" You aren't a London cab driver, Wittgenstein; you're quite probably the greatest philosopher of our time.'

'I'd rather be a cab driver,' Wittgenstein retorted hotly.

'And if philosophy isn't about life, what does it matter? Can't we be allowed to play our games in peace? Nobody expects an ancient historian to prevent cholera.'

Wittgenstein shook his head grimly. 'No, Russell, that's where you're wrong. Abstract knowledge isn't innocent. It's poison: dark, violent, implacable. It isn't merely sealed from life, it terrorizes it, it preys on flesh and blood.' He strained forward, the tip of his nose quivering faintly. 'Do you know where this terrible will for knowledge will end up? Mark my words, it will end with a scarecrow in a field.'

Russell raised his glass so as to be able to crane at his watch without discourtesy. It was long past midnight; he had arranged to meet the daughter of the new Master of Corpus in the Whim cafe for breakfast.

'What's intolerable,' declared Wittgenstein, just as Russell was about to rise, 'is that everything should be visible. That what we see should be all there is. We can't stomach that, Russell; we fight it to our last breath. Because the drama seems bungling and amateurish we can't resist peering behind the scenes for a purer, finer play being conducted out of sight. But the stage, don't you see, is bare. They came to the tomb and found it empty: *that* was the true revelation. Not *how* things came to be, but *that* they are: this is the mystery. Tell me, Russell: why is there anything at all, rather than just nothing?'

Russell squirmed with distaste. 'How the hell should I know?' he snapped. 'I'm a mathematician, not God Almighty.'

'We search for what's hidden,' Wittgenstein went on, 'dupes that we are of a dream of depth. Anything to avoid the unbearable presence of reality. If we could register that for one moment in our minds we'd be free. Or perhaps we would go mad. Instead we shelter behind ideas. Ideas! Any pig can have ideas.'

'Ideas are just what pigs don't have,' interjected Russell. 'As far as we know, of course,' he added with scholarly caution.

'I was speaking metaphorically. Philosophers are for the most part pigs. Hegel: he was a pig. They want to show that everything is secretly something else. They're obsessed with the Whole. What thinker hasn't been? There isn't a Whole, Russell; there's just a bit of this, a bit of that, and a bit of the other.'

At the last phrase Russell's thoughts drifted back to the young woman at Ottoline's. 'I thought you hadn't read Hegel,' he accused.

'I don't need to. I know what the German mind is like, I was born with one. Do you know what the German mind is? It's a blind greedy mouth which would suck the whole world into itself. It rages like an insatiable infant, gobbling and chewing, mad with desire. Philosophy is mad, my friend. We're a germ, a virus, a transcendental disease which drives men insane. That's why we must do away with ourselves.' He bent his head and looked with sudden interest at his clenched fists. 'By violence, if necessary.'

Russell fought down a pang at discovering that the claret was finished. 'I still think that this repugnance of yours is just another version of what you're fighting. You denounce ideas with all the virulence of one in their grip. You're your own worst enemy.'

'Oh yes, I know that. I'm the enemy I'm fighting. If they stood me on a gallows and hanged me I'd be happy. But I've considered this carefully. I'm not the stuff martyrs are made of. I've given my money away, I've hardly any possessions, almost no friends.'

'I'm a friend,' said Russell cheerfully.

'No, Russell, you aren't a friend. You have an interesting

mind, despite being English, but I wouldn't say that you were my friend. On the whole I find you vain and frivolous.' Russell reminded himself quietly that candour was a virtue. 'I've given everything away, but I can't strip myself of *this*.' He punched himself on the chest; Russell took it that he was referring to his body rather than his shirt. 'All I can do now is crawl into some hole before I infect too many young men. I want to find some community of simple folk who know nothing of the machine, who are immune to the virus of ideas.'

Russell smiled sourly. 'It sounds rather like Cambridge. The organic society. You've been talking to that fellow Leavis again.'

'Leavis? What could I learn from him? The man can't decide whether he is a shopkeeper or a gamekeeper. No, Russell, I wasn't thinking of Cambridge. I intend to go to Ireland, to a small cottage on the west coast. Professor Gardner-Smith's holiday home, in fact; he has agreed to let me use it for a while. I don't think I shall return.'

'You're going by yourself?'

'No, Nikolai will accompany me. He'll raise my spirits. This afternoon after my lecture Nikolai and I bought our meat pies as usual and went to the cinema. The film today was extremely interesting, and I became excited. Nikolai kept talking as usual, he can't concentrate for a moment, but I soon shut him up. We sat on the front row together as always. At one point in the film the most extraordinary thing happened. There was a sheriff chasing a bank robber on his horse; his horse drew level with the robber's and the sheriff leapt from his own horse, fell upon the villain and knocked him to the ground. There was a fight, which of course the sheriff won.' Wittgenstein looked sharply at Russell and lowered his voice suddenly. 'Don't you find that quite astonishing?'

Russell rose from his deckchair and folded it with a well-practised flip of the wrist. 'I must go to bed. Don't kill yourself yet, Wittgenstein.' He paused for a moment at the door. 'Are you serious about this Ireland business?'

Wittgenstein came towards him and laid a hand on his shoulder. 'Death or Connacht,' he whispered hoarsely.

Russell padded his way back across Trinity Street to Great Gate. Ireland, he thought to himself: land of saints and scholars, martyrs and madmen. The old lunatic should be at home there right enough.

Three

Nikolai Bakhtin was a minor Russian aristocrat and one of Wittgenstein's few close friends. He was a mountainous figure of a man with a pepper-and-salt beard stretching inch-thick to his upper ribs, and his stomach bulged through a loud check suit like a stage bookmaker's. Over this he wore a soft black high-collared cloak almost down to his feet, so that walking along King's Parade in Cambridge he looked like an outsize crow or down-at-heel impresario. His cheekbones were high, his nose hooked and his every gesture studiously histrionic. He took little in life seriously, although one twang of a balalaika was enough to reduce him to a slobbering wreck. He had been a student and then a freelance lecturer in the philosophy of language at St Petersburg University in the early years of the twentieth century. The whole city at the time was in spiritual ferment, awash with dim intimations of impending apocalypse. University life was one incessant party, everyone drunk on theoretical debate and dizzy with polemic. Minor prophets reeled delirious through the streets and shabbily dressed avatars of the infinite swarmed through the public parks. Libraries and street cafes were crammed with Rasputin lookalikes. Poets milled in the streets like pickpockets, trying to scribble their verses on the petticoats and shirt-fronts of the bourgeoisie. Great tides of mysticism surged and slopped in the city's snow-packed squares. Everyone seemed to be healing, doping, poisoning or hypnotizing someone else, nailing each other unsuccessfully to home-made crosses or practising malign long-distance mesmerism.

It was a violent time. Drunken soldiers raided hostels to torture Bolsheviks, while Dostoevskian drop-outs stalked the tenements in search of old women to slaughter. A deaf Georgian who claimed to be the reincarnation of Christ sank without trace in the Neva while trying to cross it on foot back to his digs. The whole city had gone underground. Most people seemed to belong to some mystical or political brotherhood, many to several ideologically incompatible societies at the same time. The Seraphic Brotherhood of Transcendental Vitalism rowdily heckled the supposedly clandestine meetings of the Association of Neo-Kantian Anarcho-Syndicalists. A Jewish child was found beheaded with surgical precision on the back seat of a tram. Moonfaced cretinous children were kidnapped from the countryside and carried adoringly aloft in orgiastic street parades, worshipped by self-loathing intellectuals. Priests defecting to Bolshevism met Bolsheviks fleeing to religion coming the other way. A stormy, inebriated mass meeting of students arranged the revolution for the following morning at a quarter to ten, allowing the customary quarter of an hour for late arrivals and preliminary small talk. In the city's numerous monasteries, lascivious monks lashed themselves, each other and anyone within range until the blood ran, then heard each other's confessions. The air reeked of incense and gunsmoke. The middle ground between saint and sinner had been pared inexorably away: everyone was either St Francis or the Marquis de Sade, slept on nails or drove them through dogs' skulls. Nondescript passers-by fell down on the pavements without warning, foaming at the mouth. Some intellectuals celebrated the gleaming cruelty of the machine and dreamt of a people-less future, while others strove for a synthesis between Marx and Madame Blavatsky. Creased with flatulence the city heaved and shuddered, trying to retch up the Tsar and all his works once and for all. All the world was a thought, and Nikolai Bakhtin was thinking it. He drank himself speechless every night and desired never to awaken from this paradise of endless possibility.

Lenin was in exile, but would come again on clouds of glory with the future bulging in his pocket to judge the quick and the dead. The city was stiff with spies, informers, double and treble agents who cancelled out their own every move. In his final year as a student Bakhtin had three simultaneous mistresses, a leanish period of sexual activity in his own view, of whom two were police informers. It seemed a reasonable percentage. They would poke slyly into his letters while pretending to braid their hair, ineptly memorize the titles of his books, dangle themselves naked over his recumbent body so as to peer under his trestle bed. They quizzed him about revolution with tender *faux naif* eyes over coffee so thick it could almost have stood without the cup, and slunk off to whisper late at night with burly strangers at railway bookstalls. Bakhtin delighted in this drama and fed his lovers surrealist tales of his political involvements. He told them that Lenin and Trotsky were lovers who had twice infected one another with syphilis, announced that he had copulated with Anastasia and taken part in a snuff mass with Rasputin.

Bakhtin's political experience had in fact been short-lived and unhappy. Naturally indolent, yet moved to tears by the thought of himself as a champion of the oppressed, he solved this dilemma at a stroke by joining a revolutionary groupuscule whose policy was one of dedicated non-intervention. In fact the group abstained from political activity with all the scrupulous attention to detail with which other political organizations acted, exhausting themselves with the effort of principled inertia. Most of Bakhtin's brief time in their ranks was taken up with illegal marches and demonstrations — not that he would actually participate in these, but rather waddled up and down the rows of chanting demonstrators, distributing leaflets which explained why his own group refused to contaminate itself with this reformist, centrist or class-collaborationist venture. He spent his Sunday evenings stewing mindlessly in the bath, drained by the fatigue of not demonstrating. He had joined the organization partly to gain contact with the proletariat, and was secretly depressed that it contained so few workers. It was explained to him that the working class, though in principle the universal subject of history, was in practice prehensile and warped, likely to taint revolutionary consciousness with its conservatism. Most of his political activity was thus confined to selling the group's newspaper in the student quarter of St Petersburg. The newspaper laid out the group's programme, the most prominent item of which was the building up of the newspaper. Its leading articles were given over to proclaiming the unprecedented expansion of the group itself. It was not actually true that the organization was growing, in fact it was the exact reverse of the truth; but this revolutionary lie was defended by the central committee on the grounds that though group membership was not empirically on the upswing, the unfolding of the international class struggle was such as to confirm day by day the truth of the party's line, and so made it 'tendentially' true that it was daily growing larger, even if in a purely empirical sense it was actually shrinking. By the laws of bourgeois logic the party was thirty or so individuals strong, but dialectically speaking it had flourishing branches in every factory in the country.

Bakhtin's efforts to encounter the proletariat came abruptly to an end at an educational meeting of the movement devoted to the topic of the coming imperialist world war. To his surprise, this subject turned out to be assigned only minor importance in the party's list of political priorities. Obsession with impending military carnage was the bankrupt currency of an historically obsolescent petty bourgeoisie — a gang of liberal intellectuals and religious pacifists who viewed history from a moral rather than a class perspective. Imperialist war would signify the final death throes of world capitalism, a system which dialectically speaking had been dead on its feet for a good fifty years, and so was to be welcomed rather than opposed. Alarmed by this insouciance, Bakhtin rose to his feet and delivered an impassioned address to his assembled comrades. It seemed to him, he declared, that one of the essential preconditions for the construction of socialism was the existence of some kind of material environment in which it could be created. The task of building a socialist society in Russia would be severely exacerbated by the non-existence of the country. Those who claimed that socialism could come about independently of such a material context were in his view in grave danger of lapsing into idealism. It was no doubt possible to apply Engels's case about the indestructibility of matter to the approaching world war, and argue that such a war, even if it wiped out the whole of the human race, was from a class viewpoint irrelevant. Perhaps the revolution that Marx and Engels had in mind was coming up in another two billion years or so, after the present epoch of class history had run its course and a new evolution was initiated from the mollusc to monopoly capitalism. Personally, however, he doubted that this was the correct interpretation of Marx and Engels's admittedly enigmatic texts. With this, Bakhtin sat down again and waited eagerly for his propositions to be debated. Instead, he was approached after the meeting by one of the cadres and informed that his non-activity would no longer be required by the party. He was under suspicion in any case for a prolier-than-thou rejection of its contempt for the working class, a stance which ill befitted, so he was told, a historically degenerate specimen of the ruling class like himself. Bakhtin, who tried valiantly to roughen up his patrician accent in his comrades' presence, slurring his vowels and chewing his syllables, felt particularly wounded by this censure.

For a while he considered joining the Bolsheviks, but doubted that they would ever achieve anything concrete. Instead he drifted back with relief to his old bohemian life, drank with gusto and hummed complete Tchaikovsky symphonies to admiring groups of friends. He sprayed his interlocutors liberally with saliva and spoke of a Hellenic revival. Sometimes he would appear on the street in a white thigh-length pleated tunic, and at parties he often wore vine leaves in his hair. He read his way feverishly from Plato to Nietzsche and was torn between believing every word and dismissing them all as indistinguishable garbage. He was cripplingly divided between Tolstoy and Dostoevsky: in the mornings he was neat, pious and God-fearing, cooked himself plain peasant fare in his tiny tenement kitchen and prayed briefly before an icon; in the evenings he was suave, snarling, satanic, prowling lustfully through the vibrant dark. He once turned up at a party sporting a self-inflicted set of stigmata, and tried to persuade the other guests to pour wine into his wounds. But he never suffered in his life, and was as much a stranger to psychic torment as a horse-fly. He spoke of the chastening power of great tragedy and had never even been slightly depressed. He was simple, greedy, innocent, sentimental, voracious. He did not challenge social convention because he had never had the faintest grasp of what it was. Any fact, person or event which could not instantly serve as raw material for his compulsively hyperbolic imagination he refused to credit as actually existing. He was an entirely fictional character, and the only real thing about him was that he knew it.

After a time, feeling that he had temporarily exhausted St Petersburg, he drifted to Paris where he fell in with a few painters, conceived two bastard children and almost starved to death. At this period his appetite was for drink, sex and ideas only; food he disdained as sordidly material. He spent most of his meagre funds on alcohol, which he saw as a means of direct access to transcendental truth. He would pass through various easily predictable stages when drunk, slumped at first in narcissistic fantasy, then tearful at the thought of the Russia he had abandoned, then itchy with some nameless irritability and finally fighting mad. When he arrived at this last stage he would rush out wildly into the Parisian streets looking for someone to antagonize, and after some night of carnivalesque buffoonery would awaken the next morning to find strange cuts and abrasions on his body, unable to remember whether he had been involved in a fight or for some freakish physiological reason simply bruised easily when intoxicated. Once, desperate to arrive at a party where there would be drink, he roughly commandeered a cab and realized after a few miles that the vehicle was not a cab at all but a private car, whose owner had been too terrified to refuse him. Sometimes when drunk he would become convinced that he could speak any foreign language whatsoever, feeling himself mystically in touch with the universal structure of all speech. He several times buttonholed some alarmed-looking Turk or Spaniard on the Champs Élysées, conversing with them eloquently in a discourse he felt sure they could understand.

Bakhtin's conversion to food took the form of a mystical experience. He had been starving in Paris for several days, and felt himself on the brink of hallucination. Taking his pocket harmonica he stood on a street corner and panted out a few tunes, breaking subsequently into a shambling, bear-like dance in the hope that madness might attract more public sympathy than music. He was on the point of giving up this humiliating self-display when he became aware that he was being closely observed by an elderly gentleman standing some distance away. The man was a gnome-like figure with a neat pot belly and an enormous head like the battered bust of a Roman emperor, and though there was something faintly brutal about his features, some repellant pigginess about the eyes and imperiousness of the mouth, he treated Bakhtin with great geniality when he finally strode over and introduced himself. He turned out to be English, and discovering that the Russian had eaten nothing for days swept him commandingly off to an expensive restaurant off the Rue de Rivoli. Bakhtin soon became aware that this kindness was not entirely altruistic, and was prepared for his host to turn nasty once the meal was ended.

The elderly Englishman rattled a great staccato burst of conversation at Bakhtin's head over the dinner table, which the latter gathered more from its tone than its content was what is known as a string of amusing anecdotes. He revealed that he was the head of an Oxford college, and enquired a little into the Russian's scholarly interests. An array of succulent oil-scented dishes arrived, which Bakhtin was courteously invited to eat. He picked nervously at a fragrant piece of kidney, still unable to overcome his prejudice that eating was petty bourgeois, when it was as though something had suddenly snapped in his guts. He felt the piece of kidney blunder its way down his oesophagus and loiter at the narrow entry to his stomach, when it seemed suddenly to gather resolve, burst through some thin membrane across the dark hole of his belly and plunge boldly on into the depths of his bowels. He felt an almost palpable splitting in his loins, as though some painful stricture had been miraculously cleared, and before he could fully register the sensation found himself reaching for the food before him and sinking it greedily out of sight. He could feel some great aching hollow in his innards, some immense pulsating bladder hankering for more, and reached immediately for another plate. His host appeared mightily pleased by this naked show of desire, pushing more dishes in Bakhtin's direction and sitting back to observe his handiwork with a piggy smile. Bakhtin flailed on blindly, stuffing great fistfuls of meat and vegetables into his implacable gut. His stomach seemed to have leapt in an instant from zero to infinity, transformed itself in a twinkling from the size of a matchbox to some resonant Gothic cathedral with endless vistas and innumerable side chapels. The Englishman blended wine tactfully with Bakhtin's snorting mouthfuls, intensifying his pleasure to a point of almost intolerable ecstasy, so that by the time he had mopped up the last delicious vestiges of sauce and wiped his bespeckled chops with his napkin, he sunk back like a satiated lover, looked deliriously around him and felt the city of Paris rise up, draw in its cobbled skirts and drape him about with its warm mantle to prevent his sense of ultimate fulfilment from ebbing away into the evening air.

He did not give his host the recompense he sought, and the old gentleman bore this with a courteous resignation born no doubt of many such rebuffs. Indeed he was helpful enough to remark that some teaching in linguistics was available in Cambridge, and offered imprudently to recommend Bakhtin to the Faculty. Bakhtin thanked him warmly, reflecting that to have allowed his benefactor to cock his gnome-like leg over him would have been paltry reward for what he had brought him. He sat back in the restaurant as the air outside slowly darkened through its freight of warmth, and realized with a slow stunned joy that he had finally outwitted death. If the arrows of Saint Sebastian had riddled him at that moment he would have grappled them to his body with both hands, luxuriating in their impotence to harm. His life was lodged away in some deep unquenchable darkness, and he knew it to be unassailable. There were, he thought to himself, many forms of immortality — the Christian heaven, reincarnation, composing some majestic symphony, contemplating the thought of one's children's grandchildren — but none of them could equal in its sheer erotic rippling the transcendental splendour of a good dinner. He returned to his foul-smelling den in the Salvation Army hostel, stopping to check with a passing Portuguese that he was on the right road by blowing an imaginary trumpet and beating an imaginary drum with an enquiring expression on his face.

Bakhtin took up the don's suggestion and drifted to England, stopping briefly in Southampton before moving to Cambridge. His stomach now stretched before him like a mighty chasm: he became a lecher for giblets and kidneys and all kinds of nutty gizzards, scooping up heaps of raw entrails in butchers' shops and hurrying them back to his lodging house in Mill Road, where he would fondle them lovingly against his cheek before popping them into a pan. His body was on fire for food at all times of the day and night: he would hang around hotel kitchens sniffing greedily, or stand at midnight staring like some solitary voyeur into the darkened windows of grocery shops. Bakeries drove him wild, and swam up through his dreams as images of paradise thronged with silent, white-clad figures. He lusted for the plump virgin bodies of crusty loaves, and once in a dream wrestled erotically with a giant brown crab which turned out to be a croissant. His most enjoyable eating was secret and solitary: he would bear back to his room armfuls of dark-tanned pies packed with moist pink meat and slam the door hastily, imagining that he was being pursued by the food police and had foiled them once again. Then he would arrange his pies in a pleasing aesthetic structure on the kitchen table, building them into small columns bridged by half a garlic sausage and draped with plush curtains of tongue. He would contemplate this artefact for a while, squatting on his heels a short distance away, reining in his mounting desire until it grew sweetly intolerable, and then would fall on the food with a hoarse cry and demolish it completely.

Once installed in Cambridge, Bakhtin made the acquaintance of Wittgenstein through a mutual Russian friend. To everyone's surprise Wittgenstein found him endlessly fascinating, spending long hours in his company and listening with rapt attention to his ramblings. Perhaps the Russian's buffoonery reflected something of his own secret desires, while allowing him at the same time to feel morally superior. Along with many women he was enraptured by Bakhtin's voice, a form of physical seduction all of its own, which rumbled like a bassoon but then modified without obvious transition into the lapping, caressing motions of a clarinet. There were times when Bakhtin chose his words more for music than for meaning, producing great arpeggios of gripping nonsense. Wittgenstein would sit silently through this like a man at a concert concentrating hard on deciphering some esoteric piece of music. As an exile in Cambridge himself, Wittgenstein responded quickly to Bakhtin's flamboyant unEnglishness; but his own Tolstoyan spirit could also detect within the Russian's theatricality the shape of a peasant child. There was something appealingly infantile in the very outrageousness of Bakhtin's self-display, like a child whose showing off is tolerable because he is unaware of his own ridiculousness.

As products of two dynasties about to tumble, scions of ruling classes whose hour had come, the two philosophers both paralleled and differed from each other. Bakhtin was the son of a nation with little bourgeoisie, a benighted autocracy bereft of culture and civility. Freedom in Russia prowled underground, hungry, illegal and anonymous, quelled by a brutal regime; but, untrammelled by centuries of bourgeois culture, it had not yet learnt to repress itself. The Russian censor was still a bureaucrat in an office, not the cultivated ego itself, trained to take anarchy firmly in hand without need of state intervention. Russia stifled for lack of culture; Wittgenstein's Vienna suffocated beneath it. In Russia the spirit grew heady and delirious on its meagre prison rations; in Vienna it wilted beneath the glittering detritus of centuries. Vienna was pale, obese, overheated, a cockpit of subtle lusts and artistic banalities; Russia was bleak, famished, starved of civic institutions, stretched threadbare over countless versts of ice. Only the Tsar's centralizing apparatus lent it cohesion, and one decisive strike at that would mean liberty. The spirit of truth burned feverishly through the patchy material surface of Russian life, as if straining at a thin membrane; starvation drove it to fantastic postures but could not sap its zeal, and the more shackled it was the more palpable it became. Habsburg Vienna had lost the meaning of truth, a city of kitsch and self-delusion. Nothing was what it seemed: bosom friends were unmasked as blackmailers, whisky tasted foully spiked, the city seemed plagued with a rash of wigs, glass eyes and false limbs. Rabid anti-semites were exposed as shamefaced Jews, and anti-semitism rose as the stock market fell. The houses of the bourgeoisie were silting up with junk: tortoiseshell, gilt stucco, multi-pieced rococo mirrors, multicoloured Venetian glass, life-size wooden statues of negroes. Vienna was smothered in a jungle of styles, scrolls, scrawls, arabesques, cultural graffiti, smelling of polychrome and polished leather. Everything was disguised as something else: whitewashed tin masqueraded as marble and plaster as gleaming alabaster, butter knives posed as Turkish daggers, ashtrays as Prussian helmets and thermometers as pistols. Funerals resembled circus parades, and banks Gothic cathedrals. The city was glutted with crap and garbage, screaming to be purged. Language billowed extravagantly in the literary journals, collapsing under its own excess like an imploded cream cake. The grimmer the political climate grew, the more relentlessly frivolous the city became. 'When Vienna gets gay,' remarked the Emperor Franz Josef, 'things are really serious.' 'In Berlin,' commented the satirist Karl Kraus, 'things are serious but not hopeless. In Vienna they are hopeless but not serious.' A spectacular financial crash in 1873 ruined whole families and drove hordes of citizens to suicide; Vienna's response to the catastrophe was *Die Fledermaus*. Viennese burghers swayed to blowzy waltzes and returned home to toss their children merrily in the air and infect their wives with syphilis. The middle classes grew fat and shiny but shrivelled on the inside. All over the city limbs were seizing up, vaginas drying out and penises drooping. The population coughed and stuttered compulsively, afflicted with phantom cancers and false pregnancies, awaiting the ministrations of Sigmund Freud. Vienna was in the grip of an erotic dream called culture, and Freud declared that its meaning was a repression of the body. Bakhtin's love of the senses was at odds with political tyranny; the waltzes and whipped cream of Vienna were the last luxurious wishes of a dying breed. Lacking a cultural style of its own, bourgeois Vienna helplessly imitated the past; but it banished its own psychological past into the unconscious, and Freud warned that it must remember in order to be free.

The middle-class women of Vienna wore clothes so cumbersome that it was impossible for them to dress without assistance. Viennese factory girls working an eighty-hour week slept with lawyers and bankers for the sake of a bed. A calamitous housing shortage had hit the city: people lived in boats, caves and under railway embankments, some en slept in trees. Parlour maids drawing back the blinds . suburban mansions in the morning found whole families asleep on the lawns. The public parks looked like the aftermath of an earthquake, piled high with ragged bodies. Anyone with a spare bed rented it out, and rent swallowed one quarter of a worker's income. The young Ludwig Wittgenstein trotted through the city streets in his cap and knickerbockers, holding his father's hand and gazing into the faces of tattered young men trying to sleep standing up in shop doorways. His nursemaid took him to the zoo, where the unemployed stared enviously at snoring lions and recumbent apes. There were proletarian quarters of the city he had never seen but whose names evoked in him a feeling like the zoo: dark secretive regions wih exotic creatures and pungent smells, raw and muscular like an ape's behind. There were men there who knew how things worked. His father was a millionaire industrialist, a giant of Habsburg finance and manufacture, who knew how things worked too. When he was young he had worked as a restaurant violinist, steersman on a canal boat, bartender, night watchman; he had also taught the tenor horn at an orphanage. At the age of seven, Ludwig built a sewing machine entirely out of matchsticks, and made it work. He was fascinated by anything that slotted, whirred, cranked, articulated. When he first came to England as an engineer he would experiment with kites at a Glossop laboratory and with aeronautical engines at Manchester University. There was a cleanness and simplicity about these machines, a spare beauty which appealed to his Jewish austerity. Later he was to demonstrate how language hinged onto the world, slotting together so as to picture reality in its inner structure. When language worked it was like one cog meshing with another; some of the cogs in the machine of language were idle and freewheeling, fooling us into believing that something of importance was being said when it was not. This was the metaphysical. Understanding was something you did, felt in the crook of a finger or the practised curve of a wrist. Knowledge was more know-how than know-why. There was a place in the world where all the rules governing the inner structures of things came together, and this was mathematics. Mathematics was the mother tongue of the human race, into which the whole world could be translated. It was a kind of monastery, chaste, disciplined and entirely true. It was everything that Vienna was not.

It was a Trappist monastery, consecrated to silence. There were those things of which one could not speak; indeed nothing that was really important could be spoken of. 'My work,' Wittgenstein would say later at Cambridge, 'consists of two parts, of which one is not written. This second part is the important one.' Language pictured how the world was, but it was impossible to picture *how* it did this, any more than the eye could represent itself in the field of vision. Like the eye, language was the limit of a field, not an object within it. You could think about the limits of language but you had to do so from within language itself, and this was an absurd paradox. It was like trying to see yourself seeing something, or using a pair of tongs to pick up that very same pair. Or it was like an Indian rope trick, trying to hold upright the very ladder you were mounting. Wittgenstein stood on the extreme limit of language, with the darkness of death at his back, and was struck dumb. You could show what you meant, like waving or smiling, but you could not say it. What lay beyond the limits of speech was the abysmal darkness of God, about which nothing could be said. There could be no graven image of the Hebrew Yahweh, who was beyond utterance. God was a hidden God who had withdrawn from his people, turned his hinder parts to them; there was hope and love in abundance somewhere in his darkness, but not for us. You could not speak about ethics; ethics was something you did. But by drawing attention to the limits of your language, pinpointing the places where it trailed off into silence, you could perhaps let a glimpse of what was important appear, like a momentary gleam of sun on the horizon. You could push language to the point where it crumbled, and see what happened. Perhaps it could only light up truth in the brief flash of its own self-immolation, in the flare it released by blowing itself up.

Mathematics would purge the terrible flatulence of Vienna. While Freud was listening attentively to ambiguity, Wittgenstein and the logical positivists were trying to erase the last trace of it from our impossibly metaphorical speech. Everything was to be stark and singular, pure and integral, in this Habsburg empire of cream cakes and swollen bodies. Europe was to be cleansed, disinfected, reduced to system. Giddy with its own power, the bourgeoisie could no longer disentangle fact from fantasy, distinguish a Grecian urn from a chamber pot, but Viennese intellectuals would do it for them by force. A monkish generation of sons struck oedipally against their overbred fathers. A rash of them, worsted in the struggle, committed suicide, including three of Wittgenstein's brothers. Ludwig's family home was almost a conservatoire: as a child he sat on the knees of Brahms, Mahler and the young Pablo Casals, and Ravel composed his *Concerto for the Left Hand* for his disabled pianist brother. Music had become the last refuge of Viennese scoundrels, worshipped as the very essence of freedom and feeling in a city of cave dwellers and open-air sleepers. Schoenberg scandalized the city with his ruthless systematization of tones, composing music which Bertolt Brecht described as the neighing of a horse about to be chopped up for *bockwurst.* Unlike coffee and Black Forest gateau, it was a music impossible to consume. What mattered was honesty not sentiment, a technician's tough respect for the logic of his materials. Adolf Loos invented a spare functional architecture without façades, curves yielding ground to rectangles. Karl Kraus fulminated in his satirical journalism against sloppy language. The new hero was the craftsman and logician, and Wittgenstein was both. He was an engineer, the middle-class profession nearest to the workers. Concepts were tools for tackling practical problems, not mirrors of eternal truth; philosophy was more like peeling potatoes than praying. Freud offended the burghers of Vienna less because he disclosed sexual desire in infants than because he unmasked the mind itself as open to analysis, governed by the mechanisms of the unconscious. 'About that of which we cannot speak,' Wittgenstein was to write later, 'we must remain silent,' and of nothing in Vienna was this truer than sex. The citizens rarely spoke of it and never stopped thinking about it; there was a nameless gap between the reality and its representation. Freud deprived the Viennese of their romantic idealism, as Schoenberg robbed them of their musical fantasies; beneath their capes and furs lay the suffering, recalcitrant body, an absolute limit of language. The Austro-Marxists perceived another such repressed body, the proletariat, beneath the farce of official politics. Freud would track the roots of psychotic fantasy to the body's depths, while the young Hitler, born fifty miles from Vienna and an inhabitant of the city for a while, would blend those psychotic fantasies into fascism. After Freud, it became possible to talk about sexuality, and the middle class did so with a vengeance. Psychoanalysis overheated the very psyche it sought to cure, as part of the problem to which it offered a solution.

Wittgenstein escaped from England for a while and returned to Austria. He taught as a village schoolmaster, then took a job as an assistant gardener in a monastery at Hütteldorf near Vienna. He enjoyed the peace of the monastic life, and loved working with his hands again. There was only a handful of elderly monks at Hütteldorf and a few young postulants, and the place received almost no visitors. Wittgenstein went silently about his daily tasks, feeling as though he was buried in some low pit in the earth, sightless and tasteless, listening only to the rhythms of his own body and the occasional faint sound of feet tramping overhead. He would imagine his limbs and organs as feelers unfurling from whatever they clutched, wavering and retracting until he had dwindled to a kind of Archimedean point at some desolate spot on the planet, filled with a deep delighted sense of his own unimportance. Every day he handled hoes and wheelbarrows, trimmed bushes and heaped grass with priestly attentiveness, thumbing the traces of death these things bore upon them. Each of his gestures was unique and pointless, filled the space provided for it and then crumbled away into eternity. He was freeing himself from desire, which drove men mad. The stuff leaked and dripped everywhere you looked, history was awash with it. Every object was the fruit of some appetite locked into the great empire of intentions and effects, the terrible sway of causality. Torn from some mighty dug, the human race was creased over its central emptiness like a man doubled up over his ulcer. Nothing of this could be radically altered: revolution was just another heady Viennese rhetoric, another fantasy of the doomed. There could be no desire without suffering, and desire was unstaunchable. But if only the web of longings could be loosened, causes wrenched here and there from effects, we might give the slip for a moment to that nightmare which was history.

They searched him out and brought him back to Cambridge. He stripped his college room of furniture, fearing that it might disintegrate. Everywhere you turned was garbage, clutter; the dons were conmen and charlatans, quacking and twittering, trilling with empty sounds. He began to fear that his papers would catch fire and bought a small steel safe to lock them in. Then he began to worry that the safe would rot away and threw it out. He tried to stop himself writing, for writing was a form of desire. He disliked umbrellas and armchairs because they reminded him of his body. He went to the cinema each day and tried to lose himself in celluloid. Then one day a friend took his photograph on the steps of the Senate House and Wittgenstein asked him where he was to stand. 'Oh, roughly there,' the friend replied, casually indicating a spot. Wittgenstein went back to his room, lay on the floor and writhed in excitement. *Roughly there.* The phrase had opened a world to him. Not 'two inches to the left of that stone,' but 'roughly there'. Human life was a matter of roughness, not of precise measurement. Why had he not understood this? He had tried to purge language of its ambiguities, but this was like regarding the handle of a cup as a flaw in the pottery. Looseness and ambiguity were not imperfections, they were what made things work. Did we need to measure our distance from the sun down to the last millimetre? He had dreamt of vistas of ice, stretching level and stainless to the horizon. It was beautiful, but you could not walk there. He had forgotten about friction. Back to the rough ground!

There was beauty and simplicity still, but it was not that of mathematics. It lay in the lives of those who lived roughly, ordinary people who moved at ease in the midst of ambiguities. There was no single inner form to the world, or to language. Language hooked on to the world in many different ways, from a cheer to a curse. There was no secret essence to it all, just a Babel of differences. The Habsburg empire was an ungovernable *mélange* of Germans, Slovaks, Rumanians, Slovenes, Serbs, Transylvanian Saxons, Croats, Czechs, Poles, Italians, Magyars and others. Philosophy detested all this difference, strove like the Emperor

Franz Josef to hammer it into unity. Philosophy was a form of terrorism, unable to live and let live. It demanded of men and women an impossible purity, and bewitched by the lures of its language they plunged into madness and despair. Meanwhile in the cottages and tenements people cursed and promised, wept and copulated, living hand-to-mouth without absolutes. It was this, not mathematics, which was the ultimate beauty. There was nothing beneath it; it was what it was. Those who dreamt of revolution imagined that there was some single force or principle beneath all this which could be seized on to transform the lot at a stroke. It was a natural sickness of the mind; how hard it was to accept that beneath all this there was nothing at all, that the emperor had no clothes! At such a thought the mind felt giddy, grabbing for some ultimate ground to keep its balance. Wittgenstein could offer remedies for this sickness because he was infected with what he sought to cure. He was nostalgic for the pure ice, homesick for his cloisters. He loved the common people but knew none of them. His asthmatic bedmaker snuffled and hawked, driving him to distraction. He was of Jewish descent, and from his home city were to sprout both Zionism and the death camps. Hitler learnt much from the fanatical anti-semitism of Karl Lüger, mayor of Vienna. To live and let live was essential for survival, but it could never in itself redeem the sufferings of the oppressed. For that one would need the violent, intolerable love of Yahweh, who did not exist. Like philosophy, God was a disease of the mind we could not escape, an impossible dream of wholeness. Only an implacable force could redeem the wretchedness of humanity, and this would merely plunge it into deeper misery. Wittgenstein thus turned from his father the Jew to his father the assimilated protestant convert: the only solution was to despair of history and save one's own soul. It was impossible to do this in the shadow of Trinity College

Great Gate, that monument to the arrogance of a ruling class. He would flee to Ireland, taking Bakhtin with him. He asked Bakhtin because he could think of no other man whose company he could bear. Bakhtin agreed at once, ready to go anywhere with anyone.

Four

In St Columba's church on Dublin's O'Connell Street, Father Aidan Flannery was reminding his congregation of the three dark days when Satan would be unleashed on the earth and only holy candles would burn. In a closing metaphorical flourish he insinuated a dim analogy between the unchaining of Satan and Irish republicanism. The altar boy draped an embroidered gold-tasselled cape over the priest's shoulders and scampered back down the altar steps to give three twists to his baroque cluster of silver bells, one for each sweep of the monstrance which Father Flannery thrust, cruciform, up, down and sideways in the air before his bent-headed flock. In the silence of the benediction the plod of marching feet could be heard outside on O'Connell Street, and between each peal of the altar server's bell came an order barked in Irish. Connolly's Citizen Army were rehearsing for the big one. Nowadays they drilled cheekily beneath the very walls of Dublin Castle, brazenly sizing up its ramparts. On the steps of St Columba's church a knot of young beggar women, breasts half-bared, held shit-caked whiskey-doused babies at the ready for the charitable attention of the dispersing congregation.

Dublin was knee-deep in dead babies, carried off by tuberculosis and malnutrition. They perished in droves, their livid, scabby bodies littering the city; to bury a newborn infant in Glasnevin cemetery cost a week's wages, not to speak of the price of a coffin and hiring a hearse. The tenements were clogging up with rat-faced scraps, shoeless stunted waifs. Those who survived family life six or seven to a room grew into bony uncoordinated adolescents, pasty freckled boys and gingerish girls with hunched shoulders and nervously locked thighs. A fourteen-year old girl could earn seven shillings a week working in Jacob's biscuit factory, famed as benevolent employers among the Dublin poor. Or she could stop imitating the Virgin Mary and start selling herself in the Monto, Dublin's red light district. Business was brisk around Montgomery Street, with five thousand randy British troops garrisoned in the capital. At one end of Tyrone Street the whores wore evening dress, smelt of Parisian perfume and were regularly visited by their couturiers; at the other end they wore nothing but a raincoat, absent-mindedly opening it from time to time to stimulate trade. Twice as many prostitutes were arrested in Dublin as in London, testimony to either Irish vice or virtue. A fortunate adolescent might get himself apprenticed to one of the city's traditional crafts, printing, bricklaying, silkweaving or plastering, having pledged not to waste the goods of his master, commit fornication or frequent alehouses. Employers herded their apprentices ten to a room and sometimes two to a bed, fined them for forgetting to address them as 'sir' and forbade them to marry. The odd batch of apprentices landed up in Glasnevin cemetery from time to time, victims of lax fire regulations. Girls who were neither indentured nor professionally penetrated might end up as one of the city's thirteen thousand domestic servants, or swell the ranks of its seamstresses, milliners and charwomen. Most boys would join that half of Dublin's male workforce who were general labourers, a class described by a foreign observer as 'of no definite trade, ready for anything and good for nothing'.

Ready to steal the cross off a donkey's back, they herded into the back pews of the twelve o'clock Sunday mass in the pro-Cathedral, reputedly the fastest mass in the land.

In the shadow of Georgian buildings planted like gleaming obelisks by an alien intelligence to monitor the natives, priests fulminated against the Russian Bolshevik Karl Marx and threatened eternal perdition to teenage masturbators. Half the population writhed in the toils of sexual repression, while the other half reeled around dazed from mass reproduction. Mothers worried themselves sick about their offspring: they met under the mellowly tinkling chandeliers of eighteenth-century drawing rooms, broad-busted Ascendency matrons, to compare notes on the relative merits of Winchester and Harrow. Their daughters swapped giggly gossip about the Castle's latest acquisitions: the hairy forearm smash of Captain Alisdair Bosanquet, and the lithe nipped-waisted desperado Lieutenant Jeremy Chapman. Capital of nothing, Dublin craned out towards Europe, its Scandinavian founders and British proprietors, its buttocks coldly turned to the empty bog behind it. Its signal advantage compared to London and Paris was that it was easy to get out of. Ireland was two nations, a maritime economy along the eastern coastal fringe from Belfast to Cork, and inland a rural subsistence economy where money, that newfangled commodity, was sometimes pawned rather than spent, and where spinsters and bachelors waited patiently for their fathers to die, tip over the farm or fork out a dowry. What mattered in Dublin was its extreme edge, the harbour, where it meshed with the twentieth century; what counted was what came in and what went out, not what lay within. Most of what went out went to Britain, and most of what came in came from Britain too. Visitors to the city were charmed to discover no pall of smoke or industrial quarter: Dublin was an outsize, undercapitalized village, a couple of breweries, a biscuit factory, a castle, a barracks and above all an enormous slum. Inland, the population was slowly leaking away. Ireland was emptying like a burning building, with almost half of its people living abroad.

The dead heart of the Georgian city had been scooped out and filled with living wreckage. The ruling class had evacuated their porticoed fanlighted balustraded mansions and decamped to the suburbs, leaving the poor to squat in their rotting cast-off shells. The capital was a stately brick and granite façade sheltering a scurvy rabble living amid rat shit. About forty per cent of the population were families occupying a single room, without heat, light or water. Over a third of Dubliners lived somewhere in the stinking slum which swept between the Grand and Royal canals, one half of them wearing the cast-off clothing of the other half. The Women's National Health Association, pioneered by Lady Aberdeen, wife of the Lord Lieutenant of Ireland, suggested in a pamphlet how a family of seven could be maintained on eight shillings a week, given a skilful enough deployment of skim milk, bacon, treacle and dripping. This would have left the average Dublin family almost as much again out of its weekly wage to paint the town. Dublin's workers, who could expect to live one half as long as the city's newly professional middle class, did not take this dismal situation lying down. Instead they evolved a strategy which would transform it at a stroke, catapult them at a bound into a richer, fuller world. They got drunk. Instead of suffering their degradation lying down they took it flat on their backs. The city air was a blend of stout, hay, hot pies and horse-shit, but mostly stout. Lord Iveagh, owner of the Guinness Brewing Company, produced one fifth of the world's stout there, brewing enough beer to supply two and a half free pints to every soldier in the British army. Making the stuff was even better than drinking it: the Guinness worker was the labour aristocrat of the nation, with thousands of unemployed fellow citizens waiting anxiously for him to retire, get fired or drop dead. The most revered labour in the city was that devoted to rendering everyone else insensible. Trade union meetings regularly contained their batch of paralytic brawlers; James Connolly and Jim Larkin bullied and softsoaped their members into taking the pledge, aware that rather more of the ruling class than Lord Iveagh profited from the leglessness of Irish labour.

Finbar Tierney was aware of this too, though as time went on it became less obvious. He had shown some early promise as a poet, though he had left his Christian Brothers school at the age of fourteen to hang around the docks looking for work. Since pubs were the obvious places for dockers to frequent while waiting for a job to turn up, Finbar relied for his sparse living on the fact that when work did become available a good proportion of his mates would be in no condition to do much about it. The writer George Russell came across a poem Finbar had managed to get published in the nationalist press, summoned him to his sleek mansion in Drumcondra and, sniffing thwarted creativity, swung him a job as general factotum at the Abbey theatre. Finbar found himself shifting scenery on a stage so narrow that to cross it the actors had to walk down the alleyway behind the theatre, or squirm their way between back wall and backcloth. Delirious at being transported to the very heart of the Irish renaissance, he read his way furiously through myth and folklore, studied socialist economics and brought himself a set of Greek classics on hire purchase. He taught himself to play the bodhrán well and the uilleann pipes indifferently, climbed in the Wicklow mountains and sang in a piercing tenor. The playwright John Synge once stopped after a rehearsal in the Abbey to talk to him in his intense, awkward way about the socialist ideas he had imbibed from lectures in Paris, and the poet William Yeats in his big-brimmed hat and ribboned eye-glasses, a sharp operator beneath his well-crafted dreaminess, boomed at him the odd beautifully inflected good morning. Finbar burned for wisdom and almost drowned night after night in the endless talk in the rowdy firelit bars around the theatre, throttling back his distaste for the pedantic, primadonnaish cultural intelligentsia. Their cultivated foreignness and fencing witticisms made him despise his own Dublin rasp and bullish hulk. He fell in with some Gaelic Leaguers and learnt the language three nights a week in a dingy schoolroom near Wolfe Tone Quay, along with a group of earnest young clerks, students and aspiring petty politicos.

Everyone in Dublin was an expert on the language question. The city was a cacophony of tongues, from the mincing vowels of West Britain to the thick slurred growling of the docklands, the chronically surprised shrillness of the North and the shoneens who aped Dublin Castle dialect. Some of the literati would write only in Gaelic, frightened of becoming European lest they be thought English. Others maintained that the Gaelic revival would simply make their fellow countrymen illiterate in two languages rather than in one. Some translated their own short stories from one language to the other, occasionally forgetting in which tongue they had composed the original. John Synge pulled off the rare trick of writing in English and Gaelic simultaneously, using an Irish peasant speech as no other writer had used it, and probably no peasant either. Florid-faced Irish Irelanders in green knitted ties and feathered tweed hats flung whiskey in the faces of bearded pacifist intellectuals hotfoot from Europe and dizzy with Mallarmé and Maeterlinck. Dublin hemmed and stammered away, unsure what speech to use, rusty in one tongue and humiliated in the other. Some Irish Irelanders smoked Irish tobacco only and endured the deprivation of drinking only Irish whiskey. A 'buy Irish' campaign swept the country, to stem the tide of cheap, mostly British commodities flooding the home market. A Dublin city councillor rose in the council chamber indignantly brandishing a toilet roll stamped 'Made in Norway' and demanded to know why such foreign filth was available in every public lavatory in the capital. Dark-eyed Celts, their eyes bright with mystical knowledge, boarded the trams to Dalkey and Ballybough and munched meat pies in O'Connell Street, wedded through myth and archetype to rock and earth. The Gael would save the modern world from its materialism, the last transcendental bump in the thick skull of Europe. New plays at the Abbey were rated by the critics for their PQ (peasant quality). Men who had never travelled west of Mullingar dreamed of a new Ireland of athletic young men, the wisdom of old age around the fireside, and the laughter of comely maidens spinning flax with one hand and strumming a harp with the other. Fergus and Finn, Dermot and Cormac stalked through Upper Grafton Street, wrote letters to *The Universe* enquiring after the surname of Adam and Eve, tended butcher's shops with bulblit shrines of the Virgin in their front windows. Cathleen ni Houlihan and Eileen Aroon could be found shyly measuring cloth behind every draper's counter. The hidden, chidden, forbidden Ireland was about to be reborn, an Irish Ireland whose schools would teach not only Irish history and literature but Irish physics, chemistry and biology. In the new Ireland children would be taught a distinctively Irish way of walking, sprightly, limber and affirmative as against the British slouch or swagger. The Irish style of defecation would be regular and efficient, brief in duration to avoid anal eroticism; children would be taught to regulate their bowels like Gaels, not shit as Sassenachs. All lavatory paper, like all official notepaper, would be green. Sinn Fein parades swayed through the streets, pipe bands in green mantles and saffron kilts, shopkeepers in bowler hats and tweed suits bearing Brian Boru harps, the stars and stripes, the French tricolour and banners reading 'Guinness is BAD for you', 'Ireland Divided, Ireland Down', 'A Country without a Language is a Country without a Soul'.

It was hard luck for the Gaelic League that their drive to unlock the ancient tongue coincided with one of the richest flowerings of writing in English the land had ever witnessed. The two parties clashed violently in the stalls of the Abbey theatre during the first production of Synge's *The Playboy of the Western World.* From his vantage point in the lighting gallery, Finbar Tierney watched a dozen blue-tunicked members of the Royal Irish Constabulary rush down the theatre aisles amidst the baying of affronted Catholic patriots, while more police patrolled outside the building. The trouble had started with a reference in the play to girls wearing shifts, and the protagonist's revelation that he had killed his own father. No decent Irishman would speak of women's shifts while ladies were present, and no Irishman had ever killed his own father. The West Brits were smirching the honour of Irish maidenhood once again, and impugning the morality of their menfolk. The play carried on like a dumbshow, not a word from the stage audible through the howling and braying of the god-fearing audience, who broke out into a slurred rendering of 'A Nation Once Again'. A young drunk tried to clamber on stage, keeled over like a felled tree into the orchestra pit and was promptly arrested. Yeats stood impotently on stage, flapping his arms like a great crow to pacify the simple faithful, who enraged by the sight of his pagan cravat and effete hairstyle bayed even louder. Producing a play in Dublin was more like exploding a bomb than providing an evening's entertainment. Finbar climbed down from his perch and knee-jerked a bulbous-nosed navvy who was clambering from row to row of seats, holding aloft a foaming bottle of stout and screaming imprecations. Finbar was collared from behind by two of the navvy's mates and struck out in rage, connecting with jawbone and ribcase, until the men backed off and staggered away swearing up the aisle.

Finbar had no idea why he was doing this, or what side he was on. His head was swimming with discordant voices, and sometimes he felt that his mind was about to crack. He felt a terrible slow fury burning in his guts, but it was as much for Yeats and Synge and the fancy talk of Cathleen ni Houlihan as it was for the howling gobeens in the Abbey stalls. He joined the Irish Socialist Republican Party and heard Connolly speak a few times, but there was an academicist rigour about his lecturing style which drew no response from his own inner tumult. He was finding it increasingly hard to know which way to turn. Part of him wanted to retreat into his own neck of the woods, to block out the billowing fantasies around him with a few solid Irish certainties. Another part of him was hungry for the Europe he had never seen, with its exotic commodity-crammed arcades and spacious, tree-flanked boulevards, its complex assured suavity so different from this city, where even the senile Liffey wandered about blocked between walls like a liquid highway. He was beginning to wonder whether the Irish could ever manage by themselves. At least the chinless wonders up at the Castle knew what they were about; the beauty of being a conqueror was that you never needed to worry about who you were. The Irish were obsessed with themselves, sunk in narcissism, bearing themselves painfully on their own backs like a daily burden. They hated the British but needed them too, as bogeymen on whom to project their own self-loathing, ready-made scapegoats for their own chronic failure, a highfalutin political excuse for screwing yourself up, not shaving, taking a last pint, having your spavined horse hobble in last. Without Dublin Castle they would have nowhere to locate their self-contempt.

Finbar felt his mind narrow and darken until it threatened to snap shut on him entirely. There seemed to him a terrible forced jollity about the city, as garish as a death's-head grin. Dublin was a squalid farce reaching far beyond the Abbey's walls, make-up plastered on grime, blubbery-lipped bar-room philosophers mouthing mispronounced Gaelic verse before sliding insensible from their stools, mouth and flies agape. The British allowed the Irish to play at being a metropolis, and the Irish obediently acted out the drama with all the portentous wooden dignity of a Victorian melodrama. They were like good-humouredly indulged children handed out their toys and uniforms and insignia, their false beards and glittering imitation ballgowns, until it was time for bed. One barrel swung from a gunboat in the Liffey would be enough to bring the charade to a stop, the Castle Catholics stripped suddenly of their coveted annual invitations to the vice-regent's lodge. British soldiers in scarlet uniform staggered through Watling Street with Dublin girls on their arm whom they would shoot without compunction if commanded. It seemed to Finbar that Dublin was rife with casual rudeness, hard-mouthed and brutal but also frightened and fake. Everyone was on a short fuse, tempers brittle and crackling, a slight collision on the street likely to lead to a punch-up. The Irish were beginning to detest the sight of each other, ashamed to see their own weakness mirrored in their neighbours' eyes. They scurried over cobblestones with faces averted, reluctant to look into anything too deeply; everything was slurred, evaded, skimmed, deferred, talk leapt inconsequentially from one non-topic to another and swelled to fill the aching silence behind faces. Finbar began to dissociate himself secretly from his own race, rejecting the overblown body which tied him to them. He took to solitary drinking every evening in Ryan's bar, back stiff and head unmoving, feeling the tracks of fire weave through his brain until his head felt like a purplish thick-veined fruit about to burst. One night in

Merrion Square he smashed the face of a striped-blazered Trinity College prig drunkenly bellowing 'Rule Britannia' to a darkened window. His wife left him, taking their boy with her, but he hardly noticed. For several years he had hardly even noticed that he was married. He arrived later and later for work and was fired one evening for having erected a flat upside down, window to the ground and door to the top, thus causing grave embarrassment to a distinguished elderly actress about to make her entrance on stage.

Dublin began to stir as Finbar started to lose grip. On the surface the city still went round and round like the rosary, everyone conducting the same heated arguments each night with the same antagonists in the same bars. Each day the Black Marias bumped up Dominick Street delivering their clutch of felonous poor to Mountjoy gaol. The mercy-killers in the meat factories clicked their way through the day, fell silent, then started up again. Each morning Finbar would watch one of his neighbours in Eccles Street, a jowlish shabby-genteel Jew much berated by his blowsy wife, set off in bowler hat and stiff white collar to circle the city as some kind of commercial agent, before returning each evening to be insulted again. But underground the city was creaking, heaving, its secret foundations beginning to shift and buckle. It sent out shockwaves to the West: statues of the Virgin in Kerry and Donegal began to smile and levitate, the devil appeared in a Mayo dance hall disguised as a dark young man but betrayed by a faint whiff of sulphur. Holy wells in Clare began to hop overnight from field to field. The British were growing sluggish and mesmerized, perched for centuries on this snakeless swamp where nothing took root. Their concentration was starting to waver, distracted by rumblings from their own lesser breeds back home and impending imperialist warfare. There would be trouble in Ireland if they tried to conscript.

'Enlist? Is it me enlist, and a war going on?' an incredulous young farmer would later ask the British recruiting sergeant who came to the door of his cottage. Lounging over gin in Dublin Castle, the British had begun to forget what they were about, infected by the unreality of this knockabout nation. There was something blurred and devious about the Irish, genetically bent, worryingly impenetrable. Truth for them meant not correspondence with what was the case, but coherence with what seemed the least trouble. Everything in the place smacked of something else you couldn't quite put your finger on. There was a terrible lack of clarity about the natives' speech. Most of them spoke only English but somehow it was as if they didn't, as though they were speaking a foreign tongue but oddly using your own words. This made them appear more akin and intelligible than they probably were. Their speech was English all right, but offbeam, askew, slanted, out of true. Perhaps they were mocking the whole time; perhaps this was the secret of the Dubliner Oscar Wilde with his English high society plays, a deft mimickry of English culture whose very effortlessness was insulting, a look-no-hands affair, the impudence of the circus clown who nips off with the suitcase the strong man has been struggling to lift. Wilde's wit took English platitudes and ripped them inside out, stood them cheekily on their head while keeping a straight face. Maybe all the Irish were somehow inverted. Dublin Castle's intelligence agents trailed James Connolly from one public meeting to another, at ease by now in their outsize cloth caps and soiled white scarfs, sitting on the end of a row so as to make a discreet exit if challenged about their trade union credentials. They went back to their beds and dreamt in Marxist jargon. They knew how the phrases would rise and fall, which noun would attract which adjective, the synchronized upward jerk of chin and downward stab of forefinger which presaged the passage from nationalism to socialism.

Jim Larkin had the leadership of the dockers, and held the port of Dublin in the palm of his hand. In 1913 the Dublin working class stirred, struck and was defeated, twenty thousand of them locked out by a conspiracy of employers and driven, starving and humiliated, back to work. 'We Irish workers,' wrote Connolly, 'must again go down into Hell, bow our back to the lash of the slave driver, and instead of the sacramental wafer of brotherhood and common sacrifice, eat the dust of defeat and betrayal.' It was a poetic style of trade unionism, John Synge in overalls. Military orders tended to be issued in blank verse: 'the old heart of the earth needs to be warmed with the red wine of the battlefields,' declared the republican leader Padraic Pearse, and hundreds of Irish Volunteers fell instantly to oiling their rifles. Labour leaders broke spontaneously into iambic pentameter. Dublin was dripping with symbolism: bloodstained roses nailed to crosses and watered with tears would sow fresh shoots in aching hearts. As the children of the city starved during the great lock-out, Larkin arranged with trade union families in Britain to take them in for food and a holiday. ENGLISH REVOLUTIONARY SOCIALISTS CAPTURE IRISH CATHOLIC CHILDREN, proclaimed the headline of a weekly newspaper. A handout addressed to the Fathers and Mothers of Dublin warned that kidnappers were at their deadly work. A small band of hungry children were marched down to Tara Street public baths, where they were washed and dressed in brown jerseys with their names and destinations stitched on the back. Two priests appeared, appealing in the name of God for the 'deportees' to be released. Some of the bewildered deportees burst into tears, signalling, as the Irish *Daily Express* put it, their reluctance to go to England to become English children. There was a small riot at the railway station, as patriotic parents launched an audacious rescue bid for the doomed urchins. Larkin was sentenced shortly afterwards to seven months' hard labour for seditious speechmaking, incitement to robbery and incitement to riot.

Dublin was coming awake as Dublin Castle nodded. The Anglo-Irish Ascendency class had been losing ground for half a century, gradually undermined by land reform and the rise of a prosperous bourgeoisie. Their disarray threw up many of Dublin's leading intellectuals, the swansong of a disintegrating class. Ireland had produced an astonishing generation of orators, visionaries and activists, men and women who moved from Rosicrucianism to rural cooperatives and back as naturally as their lesser countryfolk slipped from stout to spirits. Labour leaders produced slim volumes of verse while poets strode the hustings. Everyone seemed to be editing a journal or taking dictation from spirits. Each private stammerer concealed a public Cicero: Ireland was sprouting theoricians as plentifully as potatoes, men who crackled with charisma and were known as 'the big fellow' whatever their actual height, pale aristocratic women who could load a rifle and run a sanitation campaign as easily as do cross-stitch. Witches, theosophists and members of the Order of the Golden Dawn stood at night on the Wicklow mountains tracing the constellation in the sky which heralded the return of the ancient gods. The Irish were guardians of a secret doctrine, a hermetic wisdom passed to them by their forefathers. Some experimented with astral bodies while others organized travelling libraries for the peasantry. Sinn Feiners who believed that Moses spoke a kind of primitive Irish tangled with dialectical materialists who held that all belief was a spasm of the brain cells. Some like James Larkin believed with equal conviction in the virgin birth and the labour theory of value. Men and women crossed from poetry to politics to philosophy and back, acknowledging no ultimate division between these discourses. A baby born in Athy of enormous size, gurgling in spontaneous Gaelic and thought to be the reincarnation of Cuchulain, was reverently visited by a carload of Dublin intellectuals. The Irish Republican Brotherhood met secretly in a tenement room in Townshend Street around a billycan of tea, huddled over a detailed plan of the fortification of Dublin Castle. A new member was belatedly admitted to their company, the Marxist revolutionary James Connolly, and made privy to their plans.

As the city shuddered, near to explosion, Finbar Tierney finally lost hold of his mind. He was finding it easier to let everything slip gradually away. As the cackle of voices flared around him, he sank slowly into silence. One night, dazed with whiskey, he shat with exaggerated deliberation on the front lawn of a fine house in Ballsbridge, the home of a young Ascendency woman he had admired from a distance but never spoken to. It was the last mark he would leave on the city. An uncle in Kerry had died and left him his pub; he would take the boy back from his mother and move out there. He would melt slowly away into the stillness of the Kerry mountains, the means of oblivion conveniently to hand. He watched for the last time his bowler-hatted neighbour walk out on his rounds. One day the man would return home to find that his wife had eloped; he too would pack his things and head after Finbar for the west.

Five

'You must *commune* with him, Ludwig,' said Bakhtin. 'They are responsive to human affection.'

The two friends were jogging on donkeyback along a dusty Connemara road, the taller man plodding on ahead, the smaller philosopher floundering behind like some dispirited Sancho Panza. Wittgenstein, his buttocks painfully cleft by the donkey's knobbled spine, was in constant trouble with his mount. It swerved sideways like an overloaded trolley, backsliding more than it advanced. It occurred to Wittgenstein that if this went on he would be logically incapable of reaching his destination. He seemed to be wading in some slow-motion nightmare through a mountain of sand, scooping away footholds only to watch them fill up again. He glared at Bakhtin's back and cursed him silently in German. They had been driven out of Galway in the comfort of a horse and cart, but Bakhtin had spotted the donkeys nuzzling a dilapidated gate. With his customary respect for private property he had appropriated them immediately, ordering the affronted cart driver back into town. They had slung their baggage over the donkeys' backs and mounted before Wittgenstein could think better of it. Bakhtin rode along at his ease, blowing on his harmonica with tuneless gusto and occasionally riding backwards so as to converse better with his companion.

Sometimes he crooned to his donkey in low Russian and seemed to listen attentively for its reply. His animal trotted steadily along, its short patched legs picking their way with delicate precision among the broken stones. Wittgenstein's wretched creature lurched and staggered as though it had never walked before in its life.

The road sank swiftly down the slope of a cliff, dwindling to a dirt track edged by low stone walls. They came across the odd shrine at miniature crossroads, decorated with dead flowers and stumps of blue candle in weatherstained jars. They rode on past pocket handkerchief-sized fields rubbled with a few scraggy goats and the shells of derelict cabins, and Bakhtin realized to his surprise that these barren, shrunken squares of soil were still farmed. A young man in broad earth-soiled trousers was working a dizzily tilted field with a swing-plough, steering a track between the huge fists of rock which burst everywhere from the soil. He paused to rest on his machine for a moment and watch the two strangers jolt past, his face carved and expressionless in the paling sunlight. They were threading their way along the edge of an immense tract of treeless rock-strewn bog, only the extreme margins of which could be drained and fertilized. To their other side lay the Atlantic ocean, staunched by a rugged coastline with only rare spots of shelter. Behind them the Connemara mountains reared up their granite peaks, their valleys filled with gleaming schists. To their south lay the expanse of thin peat and limestone known as the Burren, bright with orchids and gentians, a place reported to Cromwell by his surveyors as a 'savage land yielding neither water enough to drown a man, nor a tree to hang him, nor soil enough to bury.' A road sign indicated Galway in one direction and Ballymeany in the other. The track swerved down deeper and the donkeys stumbled along past nibbling goats over piles of warm dung. Patches of turquoise sea glinted suddenly near to hand.

Ballymeany was thirty whitewashed storm-blasted dwellings huddled between cliffs and ocean. They clopped slowly downwards towards its tiny rectangular harbour, canted backwards on the donkeys against the steep gradient, and came to a halt under a buckled sign reading Tierney's Bar, where the village's two streets intersected to form a dwarfish square. A few mudcaked hens jerked stiffly across their path. From the doorstep of Tierney's bar a balding young man in canvas trousers was eyeing them carefully. He came limping swiftly across, his body oddly twisted but his movements neat and lithe. His face at closer quarters was grimed and puffy, with a long bulbous nose and lustreless, almost lashless eyes.

'The top o' the morning to Your Honours,' said the young man, laying a hand on the neck of Bakhtin's donkey. His voice was surprisingly deep and well-modulated, like an actor's.

The Cambridge scholars glanced briefly at each other. 'We are looking for the cottage of Professor Gardner-Smith,' announced Wittgenstein, averting his face from a sudden rancid stink of donkey. 'Could you tell us where to find it?'

'Sure I could do that with no trouble at all, you could damn near spit in the window from where you're sitting as the saying goes and a grand little place it is entirely what with the soft sea breezes wafting through it off the great ocean and the seagulls wheeling and tumbling and perching on the golden thatch all the summer through, follow me now and you'll be there before you can draw three more breaths in your body.' Bakhtin the linguist noticed he said 'tree'.

The visitors trotted on in silence behind their guide. A hundred yards from the quayside a rocky path veered off between tangled gorsebushes to Gardner-Smith's holiday home, a long low thatched building wedged against the lower cliff. The place was well kept up, though a small area of thatch was rotted and a dead dog's buttocks protruded from the wilderness of garden. Two large empty dustbins sat on the porch. Wittgenstein cast a professional eye over the cottage; he had once built a house for his sister Poldy in Vienna, supervising its construction down to the last detail. The two dons dismounted shakily from their donkeys and glanced at each other with the sudden shyness of honeymooners, as though the taller man might think of carrying his companion over the threshold.

'Come and let me show yous round inside now,' said the guide, 'and isn't it many a soft spring morning as a bare-arsed young buck if you'll pardon the language I played here to my heart's content the livelong day till the thin stars glimmered with my sister Brigid who's gone for a Vincent de Paul sister to the great city of Mullingar and it's a long and weary road from there to here to be sure and I'm thinking I'll not be clapping eyes on her soft cheeks nor hearing the lilt of her lepping laughter for many a day but that's life isn't it have yous a key to this now?'

Wittgenstein, remembering the cache for the key, tottered stiffly around the side of the cottage to a crumbling outhouse stored with piles of turf and a few mouldy pieces of furniture. He returned, key in hand. The front door gave directly onto an oblong living room, more spacious than one would have imagined from the outside, with a low raftered ceiling hung with oil lamps, a faded flowery sofa and armchairs, and a few empty bookcases along the bulging whitewashed walls. A musty, fishy, turfy odour leaked to their nostrils. The crooked young man limped ahead with a confident air, though it was the first time he had ever entered the place. Through the living room was a cramped kitchen with an enormous stove, and the kitchen door opened onto a rough path winding between clumps of rock up the cliff face. Two stale-smelling bedrooms flanked the living room on each side, the far rooms accessible only through the nearer, all bare except for a single trestle bed.

The balding young man scampered back through the house to the donkey, unslung the baggage and carried it lightly into the living room. His stiff leg seemed to aid rather than impede his progress, as though providing him with a lever.

'Now if it's food you'll be after needing, Your Honours, or fresh-cut turf or a small little bit of cleaning or cooking, Donal Tierney's the man for you I swear to God. For it's the hard life we do be having here,' he meditated suddenly, sinking into a lugubrious tone, 'what with the badness of the fishing which is something shocking and the long starless nights in the winter when the great winds tremble off the ocean moaning like the banshee and us famished entirely and huddling around the great fire of turf we hacked from the bog with our own hands and making merry with flute and fiddle though our hearts are sore as the heels of a tinkerman treading the flinty road without a scrap of leather to clap to his torn old hoof.' He paused suddenly. 'Would a cup of tea suit you?'

Bakhtin unclasped the chain of his cloak, flung the garment onto the sofa and lowered his outsized hands onto the cripple's thin shoulders. 'My boy,' he rumbled, 'it is not a servant we seek. This gentleman and myself' — he nodded in the direction of Wittgenstein, who was lying rigidly to attention on the carpet — 'are philosophers. Men of thought,' he added by way of an explanatory footnote. 'We have travelled far, from a city of spires and bridges across the sea. Tea would be splendid. But wouldn't you have a drop of something a little stronger?'

Donal grinned suddenly, revealing dark yellow teeth. 'Your Honour, is it not a queer thing entirely and set up specially to be sure by the dear Lord Himself no less that you should be looking here in the face of Donal Tierney whose father Finbar Tierney though a queer man in his head is landlord of the one and only bar in Ballymeany whose doors are open to you night and day divil roast me if they're not?'

Bakhtin thumped Donal delightedly on the shoulders. Like all pious souls he would come to the father through the son. 'Lead me to your home, my boy,' he boomed, 'and afterwards bring some tea for my friend here. Ludwig, go to sleep. Try to stop thinking. I'll be back shortly. This — poet — and myself are about to partake. I sense an affinity between us.'

Wittgenstein stared at the ceiling with scorching eyes, the imprint of a spine still threading his buttocks like a track of fire. After a while he raised his head a little and squinted blearily around, drinking in the organic society. From the river Liffey British gunboats had been busy reducing Dublin's O'Connell street to rubble. Tea sounded an excellent idea.

There were only three customers in Tierney's bar. Bridie Dunphy, raw-nosed and black-shawled, ravaged by a half century of scouring the corridors of a Big House near Tuam, sat in a corner over a glass of stout. Seamus and Padraic Nolan, brothers and fishermen, were leaning at the bar in boots and sweaters, their florid faces flushed deeper by a run of whiskies. Finbar Tierney himself stood behind the bar also drinking whiskey, a bull-shouldered figure with close-cropped hair and badly broken nose. The place was damp and draughty, with a sawdusted floor and one or two fishing nets tacked to the wall as though in perfunctory decoration. There were three rickety tables and a long bench running the length of one wall. Bakhtin was introduced by Donal to Finbar, who stared at him and said nothing. Bakhtin made to withdraw his hand after a while, but found it absent-mindedly retained in the landlord's strong grip. Finbar's mouth opened but closed again instantly before words could emerge. Bakhtin caught a quick flash of his tongue, swollen and purple-coated. He was speechlessly drunk.

It was not until he reached adolescence that Donal realized that he had probably never seen his father sober. Other children might never have seen their fathers without a cheery word or a small moustache, but Donal had never seen his without a glass of spirits near to hand. He drank one or two bottles of whiskey a day, as well as numerous pints bought for him by his cowed clientele. His drinking led to dramatic shifts of mood: on surly days he would refuse to open the bar at all, so that customers would rattle the doors and peer hopefully in at the windows to see Finbar standing at the bar, drinking steadily. At other times he would keep the place open until dawn, demanding songs from the company and turning nasty if they refused, whipping them into frantic bonhomie until one or two were able to crawl away when his back was turned and escape exhausted into the night. Dead silence had to be observed during the songs, especially his own, and he would throw matchboxes with surprising accuracy for one in his condition at anyone caught conversing with his neighbour over a drink. He was a fine singer himself, recalling the words of obscure ballads at times when others would have had difficulty in recalling their own names. But this skill made him impatient with those less expert than himself, and he would brutally interrupt anyone he thought guilty of musical misphrasing, removing their glass and banishing them from the proceedings for the rest of the evening. Certain songs contained cruxes about which Finbar was known to be particular, the sudden syncopation of a phrase or prolongation of a note, and as these moments approached the tension in the bar would gradually heighten, as the company waited to see whether the performer would give satisfaction or have his glass imperiously removed.

Finbar had come to Ballymeany from his pub in the Kerry mountains. There had been an outhouse or low-grade hostel attached to the Kerry pub, where climbers from England could rent a cheap bed while attempting the local peaks. Finbar insulted these men too, though not as savagely as he did the locals, since his aversion to their Englishness was tempered by a respect for the sport they represented. The pub was still used from time to time as a base for mountain rescue, and on one such occasion Finbar struggled into his mouldering mountaineering gear intending to spearhead the rescue party, only to fall insensible on the kitchen floor. As a child, Donal had a recurrent dream of carrying an urgent message to two desolate climbers trapped on a mountainside at the limit of their strength, assuring them that his father was on his way to rescue them. He knew that this was not true, that Finbar was in fact lying drunk on the floor, and despised both his father for his lie and the climbers for believing such an absurdity.

The English tolerated Finbar because they mistook his drunkenness for Irishness. They would smile among themselves when he peremptorily refused them a drink and mutter 'begorra' to each other, a term which Donal took to be an anglicism but which was, so somebody explained, a word which the English believed the Irish to use. Finbar was sometimes serious in refusing his customers a drink, as the pub was infrequently visited by the brewery and he feared at times that there would be too little left for himself. But the English climbers took this as a joke, even if they did not get their drink, and news of Finbar's quaint habits seemed to have spread to every mountaineering club over the water, judging by the constant influx of Englishmen who would step through the bar door already sporting the kind of wry, embarrassed smile seen on the faces of those assailed by clowns at a circus. He was local colour, and did well out of it.

One evening, returning late and intoxicated from a fair in Killarney, Finbar took his knobbed walking stick and beat Donal senseless, battering his skull and smashing his spine. Neighbours called the police and Donal was taken to the Killarney hospital, where he lay on his back for three months. When he tried to walk again he discovered that his back was twisted and that one leg was slightly shorter than the other. Finbar was arrested and brought before the court. For some reason he pleaded insanity, which Donal thought the shrewdest self-insight he had ever shown, and was confined in an asylum outside Galway. His only visitor, so Donal heard later, was a local lady of aristocratic birth, whose two concerns in life were the neediness of the peasantry and the raciness of their speech. Since Finbar was both needy and racy, he filled this bill with admirable economy. The lady had some theatrical connections, and Donal once heard it said that some incoherent phrase of his father's, probably an imprecation, eventually found its way back onto the Dublin stage where Finbar had once worked. Finbar sometimes spoke to his customers of the old days in Dublin, the Abbey theatre and his poem in the newspaper and how he had met and spoken with George Russell and John Synge and William Yeats. They listened and smiled and bought him more whiskey, knowing that he was a queer man in his head.

Donal applied to join a Dominican priory in Sligo as a lay brother. It was not a life which appealed to him, but it seemed the only alternative to emigration. At his interview he expected to be asked about his religious faith, but they seemed more concerned to discover whether he was a homosexual, and harped on this subject until he began to wonder whether it was a condition of joining. A few days after he entered the priory a fellow lay brother, slim and willowy in his white habit, leant over to him at supper and asked if he knew how they separated the men from the boys in the priory. Donal shook his head. 'With a crowbar,' the youth hissed in a saucy whisper. Some of the friars wore civilian clothes underneath their habits while others wore nothing at all. A few of them were rumoured to wear so-called flasher's trousers, trouser legs fastened by elastic below the knee which certain exhibitionists reputedly wore with a raincoat and nothing else. Donal cooked and scrubbed corridors, took instruction in holy scripture and the history of the order, and occasionally gave a haircut to those of his brethren too frail or fearful to venture out to the barber's. Sometimes a pious woman of the parish would appear at the priory door with an empty bottle and ask him to fill it with holy water. Since the sacristy was further from the front door than the kitchen, he would fill the bottle at the kitchen tap, confident that faith lay in the eye of the beholder. Sometimes he would spit in the holy water, savouring the thought of a whole family blessing itself piously in his saliva. When a tramp came to the door of the priory begging for food or money, he would give him a bottle filled with consecrated wine from the sacristy. He enjoyed the idea of the tramp passing the bottle around his fellow vagrants in the churchyard, the whole group of them pissed on the blood of Christ.

He had no religious beliefs of his own, but found this less of a problem than he had expected. Few of the other friars seemed to believe in God either. They spoke instead of the 'absolute horizon of discourse' or the 'transcendental ground of Being', and appeared to hold that though God undoubtedly *was*, it was questionable whether he in any deep sense actually existed. God was not a person in the sense of being a chap, Donal was instructed, not even a chap with extraordinary powers; it seemed doubtful whether he could be said to have powers at all, or if so only in a very queer sense of the verb 'to have'. There seemed really no way of talking about God at all, except to say that faith in him made sense in what was admittedly such an odd use of the word 'say', 'faith', 'in', and 'sense' that we could not know whether we knew what we were talking about or not, granted that talking about God was a plausible notion in the first place, which it was not.

Donal found all this reassuring. He kept his thoughts to himself and imitated the holy simplicity of Brother Kenelm, an elderly lay brother so mild, white-haired and beatific that he looked as though he had been sent to the priory from a theatrical agency. For a good two decades he had done nothing but lay out the spoons at mealtimes, shambling up and down the long refectory tables crooning some hymn to himself. If he was asked by the cook to broaden his sphere of activity to include the knives and forks he would meet his eyes in a serenely non-comprehending gaze, like an aborigine eyeing an anthropologist. Donal carefully imitated Kenelm's saintliness, and in doing so won the approval of the prior, Father Gore-Knox. The prior was the younger son of an Anglo-Irish landowner; he had been an army officer before joining the order, and had a soft unused upper-class face which radiated infinite understanding. It was said that he had revolted against his patrician background, abandoning a career of ordering people around for a lifetime of service to their needs. He did not realize that the latter was simply a more subtle version of the former. When he met parishioners for the first time he would take their offered hand in both of his rather than in the conventional one, and fall instantly to using their Christian names. But though one side of him was prayerful and ascetic, the other was disconcertingly laddish and hearty, so that Donal was never sure whether he would drift past him in the cloisters with a stately nod or come horsing grotesquely towards him, throwing punches at a dangerously low level. When he was temporarily at a loss for something to do he would appear in the kitchen doorway, the sleeves of his habit rolled up for a good set-to with the dishes. He washed up with a jovial air, like royalty driving a steam engine. If the lay brothers happened to be taking a break at the time they would quickly find him something to occupy his mind, in case he remembered their idleness in his less genial moments.

Donal impressed the prior with his piety and grew skilled in the outward forms of obedience to authority. Once he went to the prior's room up the winding staircase at the back of the priory and told him, blushing and stammering, that Kenelm had taken him aside in the kitchen, raised the skirt of his habit and exposed himself to him. Father Gore-Knox had long resented Kenelm's indolence, and was glad of this opportunity to dispose of him. The old man was shipped over to a house in the English province, where he died a few years later bewildered and alone. Sometimes when Donal thought abut the disgraced Kenelm he would slip to his room and unhook the cracked piece of glass which served him as a mirror. Raising the skirt of his habit he would contemplate his own loose puckered cock in the mirror, imagining that he was Kenelm, then jerk the mirror quickly to his face to catch the sight of his soundless mirth. He would stand for a long time in the middle of his room, moving the mirror up and down, cock to face and face to cock, his shoulders shaking in silent ecstasy.

Sometimes the more theologically progressive friars would introduce a public confession into their mass for parishioners. This consisted of members of the congregation rising and accusing themselves publicly of various sins, not usually of an uncomfortably specific kind. At one of these sessions, a young green-eyed Englishwoman rose and announced in a clear voice that she had committed fornication. The congregation waited breathlessly for further details, whereupon the young woman swung an arm towards the choir stalls and added loudly: 'With that man over there'. She was pointing at Donal. Then she added 'In thought', and sat down again suddenly. The celebrant hastily struck up the *Credo* and the mass continued. Afterwards the young woman approached Donal at the priory door and apologized for having caused him embarrassment. Her name was Edith, and she wore round wire glasses, a wooden crucifix around her neck and a pleated brown skirt like a rusty sheet of corrugated iron. She was the daughter of a high-ranking English civil servant, and had come to live in Ireland after her conversion to Catholicism. She called to see Donal a few days later and they walked together along the river bank. From time to time Edith leapt around the bank for no particular reason, warbling in a rich contralto. They took another walk a few days later, and Edith told Donal that there was a Gaelic vitality about his body, an animal responsiveness which made it a surer instrument of cognition than his mind. Since his body was in fact somewhat twisted, and since she had seen him do little but sit in a choir stall, Donal could not tell whether these remarks were the fruit of gross presumption or uncanny insight. Everything she said was bathed in a kind of high-flown ambiguity on which meaning only just impinged. They took more walks together during the following month, and Edith analysed Donal's character for him in a strange kind of imagery. Some of his behaviour was sinewy, while the rest of it was thinly juiced and sparsely textured. But he had Ireland's blitheness of spirit, the kind of feckless joy which made her warm to its people. Donal listened to all this carefully and said nothing.

One evening, sitting with Donal in her dishevelled living room, Edith steered the conversation round to the question of celibacy, scoffing gently at his dim understanding of his religious vows. Celibacy, she told him, did not necessarily mean sexual abstinence, but freedom from oppressive sexual relationships. She was speaking more softly than usual, her head to one side and her lips parted in an enigmatic smile, and Donal noticed that her knees were not as close together as they had been. After a while it occurred to him that she was asking him to copulate with her. He was indifferent to the female body, and could see no advantage to himself in pretending fondness for this woman. He left the house quickly, resolved never to see her again. But news of their relationship had reached the prior, who summoned Donal to his presence up the winding stairs and commanded him to leave the order immediately. Donal said nothing until he realized that there was no hope of changing Father Gore-Knox's mind, and then he spoke. He told his superior that Edith was a slut and a whore, a savage wanton bitch whose cock-sucking was a fine art. He advised the prior that he himself could resort to no more skilled specialist for this service, and began to detail at some length the finer points of Edith's technique. Father Gore-Knox turned as pale as his habit and sank his head into his hands, beating his temples with his fists. Donal kept on with his account in a low courteous tone until the prior rose trembling from his chair with a scream, seized him with both arms around the waist and threw him bodily from his room.

Finbar had been released from the asylum and had taken the bar in Ballymeany. Donal decided to join him, having nothing better to do. He knew that he was an unusual man, unhampered by the ordinary human affections. Unlike everyone else he knew, he believed in absolutely nothing. He had only to wait for his time to come. Nothing ever happened in Ballymeany, but his luck would turn.

Six

Bakhtin and Wittgenstein began settling in to the cottage, struggling with simple domestic tasks as they felt it immoral to exploit Donal's good will. Wittgenstein's practicality was limited to gardening and engineering; he had been waited on by servants all his life, first in a Viennese mansion and then in a Cambridge college. The two men had irritable debates about how to get the peel off a potato. Wittgenstein was depressed to find that it did not flake off under the tap, while Bakhtin thought it required steaming. One evening they cooked a crab, roasting it entirely black on the outside and leaving it raw within, later burying it furtively in the garden. Wittgenstein loved washing dishes but would do so only in a bath; on the rare occasions he was invited out for dinner in Cambridge he would insist on carrying the dirty dishes up to the bathroom, where the other guests would hear him swishing around for an hour or so. The only bath in the cottage was hung in the ramshackle outside lavatory, deeply rusted and turf-stained. Their clothes slowly stiffened and stank, and they were at a loss how to clean them. They milled aimlessly around the kitchen like two blind old crones, bumping into each other incessantly and breaking more crockery than they used. Both were daunted by the stove, and preferred to freeze at night rather than beard its baffling intricacies. They had little luck with the oil lamps either, and would sit opposite each other in darkness until the other was a mere blur on the air, pretending to perfect vision.

Finally they acknowledged defeat and allowed Donal, who had been watching and waiting, to take over. 'Sure it's not praties and the like you two fine gentlemen should be worrying your heads about,' he told them. 'You can leave all that to an old bowsie like myself. While you're after setting the world to rights in your heads I'll be fetching your turf and frying a few rashers for the price of a pint or two, don't tink about it at all.' They gave him more than the price of a pint or two, to salve their populist consciences. Donal proved an excellent servant, well-seasoned by his lay brothering. He tactfully whisked away their festering undergarments and returned them crisp and stainless. He knew his way intuitively around a potato and could cook all kinds of tasty fish to a turn. He even tackled the obstreperous garden, throwing out the dead dog and bringing along an old goat as a lawnmower. Realizing that the living-room furniture was perversely arranged for maximum effort and minimum convenience, he dragged it swiftly into more economic shape, so that both his masters could recline at oblique angles to each other, legs draped over stools and small tables comfortably to hand. He threw out the rotten half-century old curtains and installed bright chequered substitutes, rigged up a cocktail bar for Bakhtin out of an upturned bookcase and discarded bathroom cabinet, and even fished him out a crystalline decanter.

Donal arrived at the cottage at eight o'clock one morning bearing freshly cut turf to find Bakhtin snoring in bed and Wittgenstein sitting bolt upright in an armchair, rigid with the effort of not writing like a monk struggling to contain his seed. Around him on the floor were screwed-up scraps of paper in his anally neat script and some scribbled drawings of ducks and rabbits. Some of the sheets were scrawled through with angry RUBBISH! or BOLLOCK! signs. Wittgenstein, whose English was not perfect, did not know that the latter word should be plural, or that it was as indecent as it was, since nobody dared tell him.

'Intolerable, intolerable,' he groaned, his eyes following Donal in and out of the kitchen. He called him over and indicated the litter around his feet, then beckoned Donal's long-jawed face closer until he was almost grazing his ear with his lips.

'Burn it,' he whispered hoarsely. 'Burn everything I write. It's straw. I know nothing.'

Donal eyed him uncertainly. 'Sure now you wouldn't be after doing a terrible ting like that, Your Honour. Burn this stuff is it and you one of the wisest heads over the water? That's a queer ting I swear to God, sure isn't there all classes of grand scholars over there now just screaming and scrambling and poking each other in the auld ribs to feast their eyes on this stuff and what would I be after doing clapping it in the stove God love me that can't even read? I'd crackle in hell myself for it.'

'I'm not a great man,' Wittgenstein muttered. He stared vulnerably into Donal's lashless eyes. 'I'm — unclean.' He laid a bony hand on Donal's arm.

Donal considered this revelation carefully. 'Do you say so?' he asked politely. The little fellow looked spruce enough to him.

Wittgenstein clutched Donal's arm and pulled him a little closer, panting slightly. His lips were tightly pursed, and his cheeks flushed as though with some sudden inner tumult of the bowels. Donal saw that his nostrils were slightly flared.

'I am — hunted,' he whispered, in a voice so low that Donal almost fell into his lap craning to hear.

'Is that the tale?' Donal murmured compassionately.

Wittgenstein nodded and glanced instinctively towards

the window. 'They'll search me out,' he muttered. 'They won't let me rest. Each time this has happened they've flushed me out and carted me back to that infernal prison.'

'Each time what's happened?'

'This! Escape. I've run away, Donal; it isn't the first time. Once I gave them the slip and fled to Norway. I had a hut by the fjord and lived off fish. There was a young fisherman — he showed me what to do.' Fond memories flickered briefly in his eyes. 'They want to steal my ideas. I have no ideas. What shall I do if they come for me?'

'Tell them you won't go back,' suggested Donal. 'Tell them to sod off as the saying goes.'

'It can't be changed. It's my destiny.'

'And who would these gobshites be who are after coming after you?'

'Dons,' said Wittgenstein, spitting the word contemptuously. 'Vultures, parasites. They may arrive any moment. If they do' — he squeezed Donal's forearm tightly — 'you must help me. Deny that I'm here.' He gazed miserably up into his servant's face, placing his hand shyly over Donal's own. 'Will you — protect me, Donal?'

Donal understood. He squatted down on his heels before his master's armchair and took his hands softly between his own.

'Sure I'll protect you like my own blessed mother,' he murmured consolingly. 'It's a strong old gouger I am, crooked back and all. Blast me if I won't land those boyos a belt in the old gob if they try to lay a little finger on you, fine feller yourself that you are.' He glinted impishly up at Wittgenstein, who lay back his head as if in extreme exhaustion. 'Isn't it a poor old donkey you are entirely?' His hand reached up and rested for a moment on the Austrian's curly hair, tastefully reordering an unruly strand. 'Poor old donkey,' he clucked. Wittgenstein's hands closed tighter over his fingers. Donal went on squatting in front of him, squinting up at the closed eyelids, a strange smile breaking slowly over his face.

Many years later, when Wittgenstein was dead and Donal still living in Ballymeany, the latter fulfilled his promise to repel the enemy. A carload of Englishmen with hesitant manners and pink-and-white faces younger than their hair shambled out onto the quayside, made their way to Tierney's bar and asked Donal where they could find the cottage of the great philosopher. Donal introduced the pilgrims at random to one of his customers, a man, so he told them, whose mind Wittgenstein had passionately respected and who had engaged him in many a philosophical debate. The visitors were a little surprised at the sight of this local sage, who wore a tattered shirt which still bore traces of the vomited remains of his previous night's revelry. They greeted him courteously, however, and struck up an intellectual conversation in which he gladly joined, scenting the prospect of more drink. He made some general expansive remarks about the state of the world and the prohibitive price of liquor, which one of the pilgrims copied down in a small notebook. Emboldened by his success he began to croak out a salacious folksong, slapping his withered thigh and cocking his leg suggestively. The conversation resumed after a while, but ran aground on a question from one of the visitors concerning premises, which the sage took as a reference to his immediate surroundings. The Englishmen left after a couple of hours, relieved of their change.

Bakhtin had been lecturing to the assembled company of Tierney's bar on Hegel's *Phenomenology of Mind.* He took them briskly through subject and object, the negation of the negation and the identity of identity and non-identity, striding pint pot in hand up and down the floor. Jimmy Kavanagh, a shrivelled, midget-like fiddler and retired fisherman, leaned over to Seamus Nolan, deeply impressed. 'By God,' he whispered, 'this feller's clever enough to say mass.' Bakhtin drank as fast as he lectured and was soon far gone. Jimmy struck up the fiddle and Bakhtin began to perform a clumsy Cossack dance in the middle of the floor, arms folded, legs thrusting like pistons, eyes closed and head flung back. Memories of St Petersburg came flooding back to him: Tanya with her crooked teeth and brightly embroidered headband, his little brother Mikhail who had read Spinoza while still in knee-pants and who had torn up one of his own priceless manuscripts for cigarette paper while snowed up in Siberia. 'I am Zarathustra,' he thought to himself, heels pounding the sawdust, 'I am the world as Will and Idea, the bright-winged Lucifer, the Fisher King. I am Alyosha and Raskolnikov rolled into one, the ruin of all dialectic, the flowers of evil.' Tears and sweat threaded his beard and dripped from its bushy tip. 'I am the cup and the spear, the chicken and the egg, the boot and the bootlace too, I contain millions.' Thus spake Zarathustra, crouching low, legs cranking from bumslope to heeltip. Whom the gods love they madden. Flailing like a frenzied cripple he threw back his head and released the sweet agony of Russia to the rafters in one wounded howl. Seamus Nolan placed his whiskey on the bar and broke whooping into an Irish dance, face grimly set and arms pinned to sides, plunging and bucking like a startled horse. Finbar Tierney seized a bodhrán from under the bar and thumped murderously away at it with a knobbed bone. Bakhtin fell heavily against a table, rose, bowed to toothless alcoholic Bridie Dunphy and swept her off in a waltz, one arm arched gracefully in the air. They floundered together like drowning bodies and Bakhtin gazed down tenderly on Bridie's grey scaly scalp. 'My queen,' he thought, 'my Maeve of the mountain.' He broke suddenly away and leapt for the bar door, cloak billowing behind him like a giant bat. He ran along the quayside through the darkness, jumping over empty lobster pots and piles of coiled rope until he ran out of quay altogether and felt empty air beneath his feet. Flinging himself upwards he tumbled over through the darkness until his enormous head hit water, dragging his body after it. They ran out of Tierney's onto the harbour, Bridie hobbling behind with a glass of stout, to see him surface with a roar, pieces of gleaming hair forked up satyr-like on his temples. He climbed out and wallowed at their feet like a sea monster, thirsty again already. They huddled him back into the warmth and Finbar brought him a hot toddy while Bridie wiped his back lovingly with her shawl and Jimmy Kavanagh's fiddle continued to creak and swoop on the spot where they had left him, as if nothing had happened.

Seven

'Nikolai,' said Wittgenstein, 'I find your way of eating quite unbearable.'

The two were sitting at dinner in the kitchen, curtains closed against the gathering dark. Bakhtin was forking down mashed dripping mounds of cabbage, lamb's liver, potato and bacon, all deftly served up by Donal before he had retired for the night. Wittgenstein perched opposite him over an evil-smelling dish of cheese and raw onion, his sharp nose ostentatiously wrinkled. Bakhtin tilted a bottle of Finbar's cheap red wine to his lips, wiped his mouth and extracted a soft cabbage leaf from between his front teeth.

'You will burst,' said Wittgenstein severely. 'It will be unpleasant. Watching you eat like this makes me feel quite giddy.'

Bakhtin belched suddenly, jerking back Wittgenstein's head as though he had struck him in the face. 'I fear, Ludwig, that your stomach's all shrivelled up. You've a constriction there — not physical but spiritual. I was once the same.' His fingers chased a slithering piece of liver around the plate and cornered it against the messy rim. 'The Japanese,' he continued, squelching the liver noisily against his back teeth, 'refer to the belly as the *hara*. As in *hara kiri*. Their common mode of greeting is to enquire after one another's bellies. *Hara* for them is the still point, the inner centre of life. Not the heart, as in the sentimental Western tradition. When a Japanese stands he does so with his belly thrust a little forward, balancing his vital forces. To have — how does one say? — a pot belly is for them a mark of spiritual distinction.'

'Then you must be a saint,' said Wittgenstein sourly.

'The man who has belly is free, at ease with himself. He knows that nothing matters.'

Wittgenstein looked up sharply. 'What you've just said is quite insane. How can anyone conceivably hold that nothing matters?'

Bakhtin released a sudden savage yawn, discovered a blob of gravy on his beard and scrubbed it off with his thumb. Wittgenstein rose and started to pace irritably around the kitchen, unconsciously looking for somewhere to lie down. Then he half-ran into the living room and rested his head on a windowpane. Bakhtin could hear the dull rhythmic knocking of his head against the glass. He scooped up the uneaten cheese, tucked the wine bottle under his arm and wandered placidly into the other room to light the oil lamps, swaying a little on his feet as he reached to the low rafters. Rain exploded softly on the front windows and died out again. He said to Wittgenstein's back: 'I heard that Moore used to boast that he'd argued an undergraduate out of suicide by showing him that the grammar of "nothing matters" differs from that of "nothing chatters".'

Wittgenstein gave a disgusted sweep of the forearm, the rest of his body rigid. He declared darkly to the windowpane, 'A man who thinks nothing matters is a swine.'

Bakhtin absorbed the insult amicably, swinging his legs up onto the sofa. Wittgenstein gazed out through the blurred glass. The masts of a few blistered fishing smacks swayed below him in a gap between two cottages, and beyond them stretched the oily white-flecked ocean. After a while he said in an intimidatingly low voice, 'Do you mean to tell me that a man could watch a child being flayed alive, its skin ripped from its flesh, and consider this trivial? I find that entirely senseless.'

Bakhtin rinsed down some cheese with his wine and said wheedlingly, like a parent coaxing a sullen child, 'Do you know of the game Karl Marx's daughter Tussie used to play with her father and Engels? It was a kind of quiz. She would ask them to state their favourite writer, colour, virtue and so on. When she asked for their favourite slogan Marx replied with something ideologically correct — about the necessity for struggle, I believe. Do you know what Engels said? "Take it easy." Or words to that effect; the translation's a little rough.' He chuckled quietly. '"Take it easy." The old roué.'

Wittgenstein came and sat on the extreme edge of an armchair, resisting its snug depths. 'I think I prefer Marx's slogan,' he said petulantly.

'It isn't a case of preference. Struggle only succeeds anyway if you take it easy. The two ideas aren't opposites.'

'So we're all to lie back and drink and copulate like swine?'

'No, no, not lie back. Taking it easy isn't *easy*. Look at yourself.' Bakhtin fished another bottle of wine from Donal's improvised cocktail cabinet, stuck it between his legs and uncorked it with a flourish. He flopped back heavily on the sofa. 'It's a question of how one acts. All effective action is done with detachment. Not with indifference, merely with irony. If people were more detached they wouldn't flay children. Or fewer, at least,' he qualified modestly. 'Look at history. What other kind of action has ever worked?'

Wittgenstein tucked his ankles beneath his thighs and sat pixie-like in his chair. 'Nikolai, I feel inclined to say that you're talking bollock. You ask me to look at history.

Should I tell you what history is? History is a newborn baby being roasted slowly over a fire, with its mother looking on. Not once, but a billion times. A historian is one who has looked into that mother's eyes and can tell her story. If it doesn't wither his tongue.'

'I agree. That's why we should forget about it.'

Wittgenstein seized a clump of his hair at random and gave a low cry.

'To act,' droned Bakhtin, 'we must forget. What action could there be without amnesia, oblivion? If we look at history for one second we'll be disarmed. History is bunk.'

'So that's why you drink yourself senseless: in order to act. If you can stand up first, of course.' Wittgenstein stood up himself, panting heavily as though he had been running. Rain drummed dully on the thatch. 'Out there in Europe the most dreadful war in history is now being waged. I came to this place because I couldn't stand it any longer. So I'm on the run — in hiding from history. Europe is dissolving before our eyes, and we its products are simply living on a little like headless chickens. None of this can be changed. What's happened on the Somme is what's always happened and always will. Everything is exactly the way it is and not some other way. But I wish even so to protest against the inevitable.'

'Unless one protests against the inevitable,' said Bakhtin drowsily, 'one will never know how inevitable the inevitable was in the first place.' He slurped some wine and laughed softly to himself. 'You're a pessimist, Ludwig, like all intellectuals. It's an occupational hazard — the customary treason of clerks. The people aren't pessimistic.'

'The people are dropping like flies. The people are in torment.'

'If there are bodies in torment there are bodies in ecstasy. What else are they fighting for over there?' Bakhtin's voice was slurred, rotund. A gust of wind from under the front door set the oil lamps trembling, rocking great sheets of shadow over the room.

'Since the human race first emerged on the earth,' said Wittgenstein in a low voice, 'they have torn at each other's flesh with insatiable gusto. They have roasted and disembowelled their way from cradle to grave, gouging out each other's eyeballs and thrusting red-hot pokers up one another's anuses and vaginas. Can you imagine the terrifying amount of virtue it would take to quell this incessant din of hacking and gouging? A goodness on the scale of Genghis Khan?'

'That's one story. There are others.'

Wittgenstein gave a derisive snort. 'You speak like an Englishman,' he said contemptuously. 'When in doubt the English think of a pendulum. First a little of this, then a little of that. The sentimental illusion with which the liberal warms his conscience. How could anyone doubt that one sound and one only has drowned out all others?'

'There's still value; still pleasure. Love,' Bakhtin added as a footnote. He spilt some wine over his shirt-front but seemed not to notice.

'Oh indeed. But at what price? For every cathedral a pit of bones. For every masterpiece, misery. And that isn't the worst of it. I said just now that I protested against this slaughter. But sometimes I wonder about this smug assumption that it's an excellent thing for the human race to carry on. I'm beginning to suspect that this is mere sentimentalism. No doubt spiders and grasshoppers would think it intolerable to become extinct, out of mere self-interest. Wouldn't it be kinder to call the whole project off? At least that way we might rescue our grandchildren from misery even if we can't redeem our forefathers. Why not let it all pass away?'

Bakhtin held his bottle to the light, squinted at the thick end with one eye closed and tossed it to the floor. 'Why not?

Some of it was pleasant while it lasted. Nobody can cancel that out.' He reached again for the drinks cabinet, missed his aim and rolled off the sofa onto the carpet. He lay there motionless, slavering slightly. 'Have a drink,' he offered sleepily.

Wittgenstein came and stood over his humped body, his eyes flickering dangerously in the dim light.

'Nikolai, you're a swine. I have come to Ireland with a swine.'

Bakhtin opened his eyes after a while and said: 'One of us, Ludwig, is probably mad. Which one is a matter of opinion.' His voice seemed to struggle up a long way from the depth of his gut.

'You lie there like a great lump of filth. Belly! You've enough belly for the entire Japanese nation. You're a disgusting ...' — Wittgenstein struggled for an animal name and came out with '... walrus'.

Bakhtin began to croon a Russian folk song inaccurately to himself. Then he broke off and said as though he had just noticed something, 'Somebody is slaughtering somebody else.' He licked his lips contentedly. 'I think it's you, Ludwig, who's killing us all with your ridiculous purity.'

Wittgenstein leant swiftly across and grabbed a half-empty bottle of wine from Bakhtin's cabinet. He said lightly: 'I think you should drown in this.' Bakhtin gave no response. 'Do you hear me, Nikolai? I said I think you should drown in your own disgusting mess.'

Bakhtin opened his eyes for a moment and twisted his lips upwards in the shape of a slobbery kiss. Wittgenstein gave a strangled cry and tilted the bottle sharply, letting the glinting liquid spurt down in blobs and ribbons until it soaked Bakhtin's beard and formed red pools on his eyelids. A thick gout of wine hit him hard on the nose and he threw open his mouth with exaggerated relish, sucking and slurping, the tip of his tongue flickering greedily upward towards his dripping nostrils. In between suckings he began to grunt out his folk song again, drumming the carpet with his hairy fists, his eyes fixed mockingly on his maddened colleague.

'Swine', panted Wittgenstein, 'filthy walrus swine.' The bottle emptied with a dull gurgle and he caught a flash of Bakhtin's bared belly, a crinkled hillock of flesh protruding between trousers and shirt. Fixing his eyes firmly on this target he seized the bottle by its neck and swung it high about his head. As he did so the cottage door burst open and a voice shouted harshly: 'Stand still there now!'

Wittgenstein turned on the spot, bottle frozen in mid air, to see a curly-haired young man in a long trenchcoat standing in the doorway. He was pointing a revolver at Wittgenstein's head.

'In the name of the Irish republic,' the curly-haired stranger added.

Behind his shoulder a smaller, older man had appeared in the doorway, unshaven, also wearing a trenchcoat. He was on crutches but his right hand cocked a revolver. Wittgenstein dropped the bottle and stared down wildly on his supine friend.

'Nikolai,' he screamed, 'they have come to take me!'

Bakhtin raised his head slowly and gazed at the man on crutches. 'The wounded Christ!' he exclaimed softly, letting his head hit the floor again with a thud.

Eight

Connolly had escaped south from Dublin in the company of three officers of the Irish Citizen Army. Behind them the General Post Office in O'Connell Street, headquarters of the insurgent republican forces, was ablaze from shells fired by British guns stationed at Trinity College, and by an Admiralty vessel which had entered the river Liffey. The British were once more busy demolishing their own empire. Connolly, who had held that no capitalist nation would engage in the wholesale destruction of property, had been proved mistaken.

Dublin was in flames, and the fire brigade was unable to venture out for fear of getting shot. As O'Connell Street crumbled, the republican fighters warrened it from end to end, tunnelling their way to safety through the walls of shops and houses. Connolly, surrounded by burning buildings and a hail of gunfire, had been directing the building of a barricade outside the GPO when he stopped in mid-order, paused, then resumed command in the same voice. He had been shot in the arm, and wanted to conceal the fact from his troops. Later his left ankle was shattered by a dumdum bullet, and he managed to crawl back inside the post office. After a hasty operation on his foot he lay in a bed on the ground floor of the building, directing operations and reading a detective story in his calmer moments.

Finally the post office was evacuated and Connolly was brought out on a stretcher, a young boy from the republican youth movement running alongside him to shield his body from the gunfire. Padraic Pearse, president of the provisional government, stood in the street indifferent to bullets, supervising the evacuation. Thousands of British reinforcements were pouring into the capital, and their artillery was getting ready to shell an area of the city which contained hundreds of civilians. The republican army council convened hastily, decided to surrender and sent out a soldier with a white flag, whom the British promptly shot. Two more men with white flags were also shot by snipers. Finally a young nurse, Elizabeth O'Farrell, walked out onto O'Connell Street waving a white flag high over her head, and was received by the British Commandant.

Whoever speaks of a pure revolution, remarked Lenin when he heard of the Easter Rising, will never live to see it. He could say that again. It had been a rough-and-ready sort of insurrection, distinctly unclassical. Most revolutions turn around place names resonant with glamour: the Winter Palace, the Père Lachaise, the Place de la Bastille. The Dublin uprising took place not on the pure ice of the Winter Palace but on the rough ground of Jacob's biscuit factory and Noblett's sweet shop at 34 O'Connell Street. There was a gap between this unepical terrain and its representation in myth and legend. A stream of mutually conflicting orders issued before the event ensured that only a small fraction of the Irish Volunteers knew that the revolution was on. Most of them heard about it later, and wondered why they had not been told. The uprising outside Dublin was a fiasco. A German vessel bearing a cargo of obsolete arms for the rebels sailed into Tralee Bay to find nobody to meet it; there had been a mistake over the date of its arrival. Hanging around for a rendezvous, the ship was spotted by British warships and promptly scuttled itself, leaving the south and west of the country without arms. Sir Roger Casement, republican link man with Germany, stepped ashore out of a German submarine and was almost instantly arrested. The rising went ahead anyway. Members of the Citizen army from all over Dublin, some still grimed from factory work, others dripping from having swum the canal, converged on Liberty Hall in response to the mobilization order. The republican John MacBride had heard nothing of the planned insurrection, but happened to be in Dublin at the time attending a wedding and cheerfully joined in. He was the husband of the Fenian Maud Gonne, by the light of one tress of whose hair it was said men could thresh out a full barn of corn on a dark night. Several members of the Abbey theatre company, gathered to rehearse Yeats's nationalist play *The Countess Cathleen*, transferred the drama to the streets by joining in the rebellion. In an improvised piece of street theatre, Padraic Pearse read out the proclamation of the provisional government from the steps of the Post Office, to the ragged applause of a group of largely uncomprehending bystanders. The proclamation was to be posted around the city centre, but someone had forgotten the paste. Flour was commandeered from a baker's shop, and a group of twenty men with a handcart trundled around the city centre posting up the call to arms.

Hardly anybody responded to it. Life in the capital continued much as usual, with people clocking on for work and drinking in the bars while the revolution went on round the corner. Everything, it seemed, continued exactly as it was and not some other way. The *Irish Times* went on being published. People still moved fairly freely at first in the city centre, hampered only by the odd barricade and the occasional sniper's bullet. The only anti-capitalist activity on the citizenry's part was looting. Seizing advantage of the disarray in O'Connell Street, tattered urchins staggered out of shop doorways bearing cartons of chocolate bars and carried them off triumphantly to the tenements. Their elders sat placidly on the pavements trying on boots and shoes. A few young women undressed entirely in shop windows, adorning themselves with silk knickers and undervests. The Volunteers, holed up in their look-out posts, fired the odd disgusted shot over their unpatriotic countryfolk's heads, while the looters shouted back threats and insults: 'Wait till the Tommies get you, you Fenian bastards!' The revolution, as it had promised, had brought wealth and liberty to the people: the Dublin slums were awash that week with fur coats and jewellery, luxury foods and crates of whiskey.

The Citizen Army wasted valuable time digging trenches in Stephen's Green, apparently oblivious of the fact that it was overlooked by buildings on all four sides. The dour Irish-Spaniard Eamon de Valera, tall enough to have been described as looking like something uncoiled from the Book of Kells, was covering with his troops the main road from Dun Laoghaire along which soldiers landing from England would have to pass. Into his view tottered a company of the Dublin Veterans Corps, a pro-British body composed largely of elderly dons from Trinity College. They were known as the Gorgeous Wrecks, after the *Georgius Rex* initials on their armbands, and carried rifles but no ammunition. To their surprise the Wrecks came under fire from Dev's men, and five of them fell dead. A dozen republican fighters on Mount Street bridge held up the advance of British reinforcements from Kingstown for a whole day, as several companies of Sherwood Foresters hurled themselves repeatedly and unavailingly against their gunfire. A Dublin nurse liberal-mindedly tending wounded British soldiers in the street was later awarded the Military Medal for bravery and a part in a West End review called *Three Cheers* at the Shaftesbury theatre. Men of the South Staffordshire regiment, hampered by the presence of non-combatants in engaging the rebel forces, ran amok and broke down the doors of homes. They threw children down flights of stairs, beat their mothers unconscious and bayoneted their fathers. It was a rough-and-ready revolution. When the Irish Volunteers were led away to prison, to the jeers and catcalls of the citizens for whom they had fought, over one thousand three hundred people in the city had been killed or seriously wounded. Two thousand Irishmen and women were shipped without trial to internment camps in Britain; ninety of the insurgents were tried by secret court martial and sentenced to death. 'Have you heard the news?' asked a delighted Countess Constance Markievicz of a fellow prisoner in Kilmainham gaol. 'I have been sentenced to death!' She had run the soup kitchens during the 1913 lock-out which brought Dublin to a standstill, had formed and trained the republican youth movement, wore her own female version of the Citizen Army uniform and later, her death sentence commuted, was to be elected on the Sinn Fein ticket as Britain's first woman MP. As the dispirited rebels were being led away by British soldiers in O'Connell Street, the lone voice of a Dublin shop girl was heard to ring out clearly from the crowd: 'Long live the republic!' John Redmond, leader of the Irish parliamentary party at Westminster, pronounced his patriotic 'detestation and horror' at the news of the rebellion. A singer in a London club hastily altered the last line of his song to 'When British eyes are smiling'. The American press, with touching faith in English traditionalism, recorded that the leaders of the uprising had been imprisoned in the Tower of London. The poet William Yeats, enjoying a holiday abroad at the time, was informed about the event and was furious that he had not been consulted.

Connolly and his men arrived exhausted in Galway to find the insurrection there too in pieces. Liam Mellowes, the local commandant, had led a thousand men in destroying bridges, cutting telephone wires and attacking barracks. They captured the town of Athenry but were encircled by British troops. Mellowes decided to stand and fight but priests persuaded his men to disperse, and Mellowes took to the hills. Connolly took shelter at first in the house of a young schoolteacher, but Galway was becoming too hot to hold him. He and a young officer of the Galway Volunteers, Kevin Molloy, were driven out by night to Ballymeany, where Professor Gardner-Smith's cottage was thought to be standing empty. The driver returned to town to organize what reinforcements he could from the wounded or fleeing rebels to go out to the village and protect the Commandant-General.

Connolly interrogated the two foreigners and felt satisfied with their account of themselves, while Molloy frisked them thoroughly and searched the house. He was a good soldier, Connolly thought, though perhaps a shade too honourable to be entirely reliable in a crisis. Connolly lay on the sofa, propping his wounded foot on a cushion, while Bakhtin and Wittgenstein stood against a wall as Molloy had instructed them. Wittgenstein stared icily at the recumbent Connolly, his body still trembling from the invasion of Molloy's hands, and snapped: 'You'll find nothing here. There's nothing valuable in the place.'

'We're not robbers,' Connolly replied curtly. 'It's shelter we need. We have to stay here for a while. You won't leave this place while we're here.'

Molloy came in from searching the bedrooms and said to Connolly: '*B'fhéidhir linn iad do coimeád mar gialla; fir tábhachtacha iad.*'

Connolly replied: '*B'fhéidhir é. Ach is sibhialtaigh agus strainséiri iad. Bheadh droch-chuma air*'. [We could hold them hostage; they are important men. Perhaps. But they are civilians and foreigners. It would look bad]. 'He says,' he explained, 'that as long as you're peaceful no harm will come to you. If you try to leave the cottage you'll be shot.'

Bakhtin pointed suddenly to Connolly's foot and said, as though drawing his attention to something he had overlooked, 'You're injured.'

'Yes. I was shot in Dublin. A bullet struck the pavement and ricocheted into my foot.'

'A bank robber, perhaps?' enquired Bakhtin, scenting adventure.

Connolly eyed him with faint surprise. 'You haven't heard of the events in Dublin?' Then, seeing their blankness, 'There's been an uprising against British rule. The post office and some other buildings were seized. There was a good deal of shooting.'

'And you were caught up in the fighting?'

'I was Commandant-General of the insurgent forces.'

Bakhtin and Wittgenstein looked at each other in astonishment. 'You're a ... rebel?' Wittgenstein asked him. Memories of the discontented Irish stirred dimly in his mind.

'I'm a republican, yes.'

'Was the uprising successful?' asked Bakhtin. He was eager to know whether he was in the presence of a world-historical figure.

'That remains to be seen. The insurgency itself failed, but that we'd expected. I ordered my troops to surrender because the enemy forces were about to set fire to civilian homes.'

'But the fighting's still going on?'

'No, it's ended for the moment. It'll start again once the British begin to execute the military leaders. Then the Irish people will rise up.'

Wittgenstein looked irascibly at Connolly, as though stung by a callowly dogmatic student. 'How can you possibly know such a thing?' he snapped. 'How long have the British been in your country, may I ask? Several centuries, I believe. And you expect to undo all that with a street riot?'

'You believe that force will achieve your ends?' Bakhtin enquired politely.

Connolly gestured to his injured leg and said with a faint smile: 'I'm certainly no stranger to violence.'

'Then you're using the enemy's weapons,' said Bakhtin. 'No good can ever come of that.'

'If we succeed it won't be in the first place by shooting, but by being shot. The ruling class can only understand victory. They underestimate the power of failure.'

'You mean you intended to fail?'

'Failure is a condition with which the working class is familiar. They have the edge over their rulers there.'

'But not, alas, in military expertise.'

'That's true. The reluctance of oppressed people to resort to arms has always contrasted with the readiness of their rulers to shed blood.' He looked across at Molloy, who had taken up a position by the window, one leg on a chair, from which he could look outside yet cover the room. 'You'll go to bed now. Remember that if you try to escape during the night we shall shoot you.' He said it in the tone of a host reminding his guests where the bathroom was.

Bakhtin and Wittgenstein retired to their bedrooms, accompanied by Molloy. He re-checked the windows of their rooms to ensure that they were too small to squeeze through. Then he came back into the living room and resumed his post by the window.

'The lads should be here by dawn,' he remarked to Connolly.

'Yes,' said Connolly. But what if they're not, he thought to himself. He closed his eyes and tried to ignore his inflamed leg.

Donal limped his way lightly through the front door the next morning, clutching a roll of linoleum to brighten up the kitchen. He felt a sudden unfamiliar pressure between the bones at the back of his neck and dropped the linoleum with a startled croak.

'You see what this is now? You see it, do you?' Molloy showed him the gun and clapped it to his face. 'Now you do what you have to here, do you hear me, but don't you stir from this place. If you try to run I'll blow a big hole in this.' He tapped Donal softly on the skull with the muzzle of his revolver. Donal looked in bewilderment at his two masters, who were sitting mute, eyes averted, in their adjacent armchairs, then stared at the stranger on the sofa. His eyes met Connolly's and his mouth fell slackly open.

'Holy Mother of God,' he whispered. 'It's Himself.'

Molloy thrust him out into the kitchen and closed the door behind him. While Donal was searched and interrogated, Connolly sat with his head slightly cocked, as though listening for sounds from the outside. His unshaven jaw worked up and down a little, and there was a crease of pain or concentration from his hairline to the root of his nose. Bakhtin noticed that he had a slight squint. Connolly became aware that he was being scrutinized and said, as if to explain his tenseness, 'We're expecting reinforcements from the town. They should be here sometime this morning.'

'Reinforcements for what?' asked Bakhtin.

'For me. To protect me.'

'From the British?'

Connolly nodded. 'They'll be here sooner or later. They're searching the entire country.'

'And what will you do when they arrive?'

'Give myself up. What else can I do?'

'Why bring reinforcements if you intend to surrender?'

'There's no point in surrendering straight away. We'll put up a bit of a fight first.'

Bakhtin pondered this for a moment, brow puckered. 'If

you intend to surrender in the end, why not do so now and save yourself trouble? Why keep running away if they'll catch you sooner or later?'

'I'm not running away. It's just that later is better than sooner. The longer I'm at large the longer our cause will be kept alive.'

'And what will the British do with you when they find you?'

'Shoot me.'

Bakhtin lowered his voice respectfully, like a man suddenly advised that he is in a funeral parlour. 'You don't expect to live?'

'I hope not to. Once the British shoot us they're done for.'

'Are we to take it,' Wittgenstein asked haughtily, 'that you're intent on becoming a martyr?'

'That's right.'

Wittgenstein stared violently into his left cuff and clutched a chunk of hair with his right fist.

'We Irish don't regard the condition as particularly unusual,' Connolly continued. 'There's an ancient tradition of hunger striking in this island. If a tenant was dispossessed of his cabin and land he might go and starve to death on his landlord's doorstep.'

'Where I come from,' said Wittgenstein tartly, 'that's known as suicide. I take it that this rebellion of yours has the blessing of the Pope?'

'I don't take my politics from the Pope, any more than I take my economics from the book of Isaiah.'

'That's fortunate. I can think of precious little in the New Testament to support Irish republicanism.'

'And I can find precious little to support British imperialism.'

'You must forgive me,' said Bakhtin, a touch of mischief lightening his voice. 'I'm a stranger to these matters. Where

I come from the priests regard socialists as the spawn of Satan, and the socialists want nothing better than to hang the clergy from their own belfries. Perhaps you manage things differently over here.'

'If God exists,' remarked Wittgenstein, 'then he lies beyond our speech. Beyond politics too.'

'That's the view of an Archbishop,' said Connolly curtly. 'The God of Abraham is a political God. He cares that the poor are protected from the violence of the rich, not about burnt offerings.'

Bakhtin cocked his head wickedly. 'And his injunction against stealing? Isn't this God of yours a little too preoccupied with private property for a good socialist?'

'The stealing in question has nothing to do with private property. It concerns kidnapping — the stealing of men. One tribe would steal the able-bodied young men of another tribe for slaves.'

'Isn't it queer,' said Wittgenstein, 'that you detest the British empire yet cling to an institution steeped a thousand times deeper in blood? A gang of butchers and terrorists who learned nothing from the death of their leader but how to exterminate? Their sole original contribution to history is that they do so in the name of love.'

'I don't deny this.'

'I'm not concerned with whether you deny it. I'm concerned with your answer to it.'

'I have no answer. The church is imperfect, like all institutions.'

'That,' said Wittgenstein coldly, 'is the most banal hypocrisy I've heard for the last ten years, most of which have been spent in the university of Cambridge.'

Molloy entered suddenly from the kitchen, munching a sandwich. He jerked his thumb in the direction of the invisible Donal. 'He's making breakfast, sir. Should I stay with him now?'

'No, leave him be. Cover the window. Is there no sign of the lads?'

Molloy crossed to the window and pushed back the curtains. By craning his neck he could glimpse a patch of the road leading into the village past Tierney's bar. Down below him on the net-strewn quayside a knot of middle-aged overweight fishermen, bellies bulging through their soiled white sweaters, were horsing aimlessly around among the lobster pots. Molloy shook his head, thrust his revolver into his belt and pulled out a cigarette.

Bakhtin said in a tone of courteous commiseration: 'It seems your reinforcements haven't arrived.'

Connolly made no reply. Bakhtin was beginning to find the atmosphere of the cottage a little grim. He thought wistfully of Tierney's bar; perhaps Connolly and Molloy would let him slip out later for a quick one. Wittgenstein was staring rudely at Connolly, itchy and inquisitive. As a man who believed passionately in equality but felt superior to everyone, he was having trouble in taking the Irishman's measure. He had just been on the point of flattening him when his loutish companion had intervened. He tried again.

'How can you be so certain that this insurrection of yours will succeed?'

'I know the Irish people,' replied Connolly. 'I also know the British army. I was a soldier in their ranks when I was young. They're far from invincible.'

'They don't seem to have fared too badly in Dublin.'

'The great only appear great because we're on our knees. The people will rise up because however much they fear revolution they won't stand for their countrymen being shot for their love of Ireland.'

'Revolutions,' said Wittgenstein, 'are of two kinds. Those that leave everything exactly as it was, and those that make it a good deal worse. Which variety is yours?'

'A successful one, I hope. Like the one which produced you.' Wittgenstein stared blankly. 'I mean the bourgeois revolution.'

'You call that successful?'

'Of course. So much so that we've all quite forgotten it ever happened.'

'You believe revolution in this country is realistic?'

'I'm a revolutionary because I'm a realist. I've never been able to swallow the fantasy that parliamentary democracy or a few more bags of grain might set the world to rights. It's crisis which is common in this country, not tranquillity.'

'While the revolutionary leaders speak of crisis,' said Wittgenstein, 'everything for the common people carries on just as it was.'

'The fact that everything carries on just as it was,' replied Connolly, '*is* the crisis.'

'Bollock,' said Wittgenstein. 'The people live on in the simple self-evidence of their lives. It's philosophers like yourself who would pitch them into a state of emergency.'

'An oppressed people knows that every moment is a state of emergency. It's only ruling classes who can afford to view such situations as untypical. What we have now is disorder, into which revolution seeks to introduce some stability. Revolution isn't a runaway train; it's the application of the emergency brake.'

Bakhtin released a sudden chuckle. 'You speak like a true Bolshevik, my friend. You seek stability, just like the reactionaries you oppose.' He rose with a grunt from his armchair and stood looking down at Connolly, thumbs hooked in his voluminous check trousers. 'Stability, I fear, is an overrated virtue. What interests me more is the nature of this little game you and your friends have been playing in Dublin. You rise up, though you know you can't win. You fight, but you don't hope to succeed. You're on the run, but not running away. That strikes me as magnificent. I find its incoherence quite entrancing. It's a kind of theatre — a charade. To know that death is inevitable yet still to dance, still to revolt, still to give bread to a beggar. That is the purest freedom possible. I bow to your uprising.'

'Don't be frivolous, Nikolai,' Wittgenstein muttered.

'No,' said Connolly mildly, 'what he's just said doesn't strike me as frivolous. On the contrary, there's much truth in it. But you misunderstand us even so. We didn't revolt just for the sake of it. That would surely be immoral — for me as Commandant to throw men pointlessly before British guns. I'm not in the business of sending lambs to slaughter; that's why our action was called off. A blood sacrifice is necessary if we're to achieve our goals, but that's a tragedy, not something to be celebrated. It wasn't of our choosing.'

'The splendour of your action, my dear sir,' muttered Bakhtin, running his fingers softly through his beard, 'evaporates as soon as you speak of goals. You yourself have said that the significance of your rebellion lies in failure. Once you talk of achievement you become a prisoner of the very rhetoric you oppose. That's why you talk of tragedy. Forget about tragedy, my friend; it's a conspiracy of the rich, designed to keep the rest of us in our places. It seems to me that you've just taken part in the most glorious comedy.'

Molloy said harshly from his look-out post: 'You wouldn't say that if you'd seen the corpses in O'Connell Street.'

'I thought,' said Bakhtin mollifyingly, 'that a corpse was what you Christians worshipped.'

'Your theology is a little awry,' said Connolly dryly. 'At the centre of the Christian faith is indeed a dead body, but one whose failure heralds resurrection. In this sense you're right about the comedy; you just locate it in the wrong place. Comedy is what comes in the end.'

'As long as you believe that,' replied Bakhtin, 'I'm afraid

you will never be free. What kind of revolutionary is it whose laughter is always deferred? When you threw prudence to the winds and rose up with no chance of victory, then you were free. Now history has overtaken you again. You seem somehow to have missed the meaning of your own rebellion. What you've described as having happened in Dublin is a kind of fiction. Now you're beginning to mistake that fiction for reality.'

'There are certainly many fictions in this country,' said Connolly. 'You have something there. We Irish are no strangers to symbolism, but symbolism in itself will leave us an occupied land. It's insurrection which the British find offensive, not the crucifix or the shamrock.'

Donal put his head around the kitchen door. 'If your Honours'll be after eating breakfast it's all ready for you,' he announced humbly. 'Rashers, taties, sassage, toast, and the tea's wet.' He gazed with fascination at the man on the sofa, like an Untouchable finding Gandhi at his elbow.

'Bring some rashers in here to me,' ordered Connolly, 'and give some to the lieutenant here.' Bakhtin rose eagerly, snuffling the warm scent of sausage wafting in from behind Donal's head. Wittgenstein sat motionless, without desire. Donal turned at the kitchen door and said to Connolly: 'Sure and won't it be an honour to serve you sir what with you and your fine brave lads spilling your blood for the auld country and kicking the craven Sassenach into the ocean like Brian Boru did before us and if it's strong limbs and a true heart you're after Mr Connolly Donal Tierney's your man divil fry me if he isn't Ireland her own and ourselves alone and a nation once again and I'm thinking you'll be finding none in the length and breadth of Ballymeany more sprightly to load a musket for the grand old cause than meself God blast me if you would.' He closed the kitchen door softly behind him.

Connolly looked up at Bakhtin and Wittgenstein, his lips

twitching slightly. 'Which of you,' he asked, 'has been instructing that fellow in stage Irish?'

Bakhtin raised his arms towards the ceiling. 'Mr Tierney is a poet. A wordsmith, like all of your people.'

Molloy spoke flatly through his cigarette. 'Poet my arse. That gobshite's as crooked as a donkey's leg.'

'What did I tell you?' asked Bakhtin delightedly. 'A people to whom metaphor is natural.'

'We were speaking about fictions,' said Connolly. 'You've just witnessed one of them. The Irish are an illusion: an invention of the British. The feckless Mick, part poet, part child, part savage. The Calibans of the United Kingdom. Some of our people believe this myth themselves; others find it convenient to act it out. This country is full of stage Irish, not to speak of the supporting cast of thousands in London and Liverpool.'

'At least they have the better of the English,' said Bakhtin. 'The English have no mythology worth speaking of.'

'Not at all. The British have a myth of themselves, which the Irish have helped to create. They believe themselves to be cool, practical, phlegmatic. This is just a disguise for dealing with their colonials. In reality they're muddle-headed, emotional and incapable of running a pig farm.'

Bakhtin, torn painfully between sausage and intellectual debate, compromised by pausing for a moment at the kitchen door. 'You should remember that myths have much truth about them,' he warned Connolly benignly. 'Your people aren't savages, but they are warriors, spirited where the English are spineless. You should cherish such fictions, not scorn them.'

'That's nonsense,' said Connolly. 'Another British invention. The Irish aren't a violent people. When did they last rise *en masse* against their oppressors? Over a century ago. It's the British who pride themselves as compromisers and never fail to raze a city to the ground when their profits are threatened.'

Bakhtin bowed deeply and passed into the kitchen. Wittgenstein sat on silently, trying to decide whether he admired the man on the sofa more than he detested him. Connolly's moral absolutism struck him as both appalling and appealing. He tried to settle the issue by another question.

'What it is exactly about the British occupation of your country which makes you feel justified in violent rebellion?'

Connolly settled his head back wearily on a cushion and closed his eyes. His left leg felt monstrously swollen to the top of the thigh, drumming and twitching with an intricate life of its own. He wondered whether he had anything to say to the bad-tempered upper-class don before him. He had already let himself be tempted further into argument than he wanted. It was the old rhetorical weakness Lillie used to tease him with. 'Sure you'd be jawing about Marx and Aquinas while the Tommies were carting you off to gaol,' she had told him, years ago when he was organizing workers in Newark. It had almost happened too. There was the police sergeant in Chicago to whom he had slipped a pamphlet by Engels while in custody, a decent man with no illusions about his superiors. Never lose an opportunity to educate. And what else did the Irish have but blather and blarney, he thought to himself bitterly; what else was left to a race bereft of its history? A colonial territory was a land where nothing happened, where you reacted to the narrative of your rulers rather than created one of your own. Nothing could grow in this stony soil; the West was empty, great tracts of rocky void. Meanwhile you talked, in the bars and pulpits and political meetings, at the race track and in bed and the back pews. Talk came out and drink went in, both dream machines, both devices for doing nothing century after century. Yet talk was a kind of action, unlike drink. Discourse was something you did: it could gather ten thousand armed men on the streets, unionize dockers, convert an aristocrat to a Fenian. The Irish had never fallen for the English myth that language was a second-hand reflection of reality. Laurence Sterne had exploded that fallacy in an orgy of laughter. For Swift and Burke and O'Connell rhetoric was as real as a rifle: it could clothe children and console the dying, banish typhoid and purify the coinage. Language was both sickness and cure, the last freedom left to a demoralized land.

Never lose a chance to educate. Lillie had taught him spelling and punctuation, checking his early newspaper articles and tutting over his casualness with the semi-colon. Born in the Cowgate area of Edinburgh, he had left school at the age of eleven and started work as a compositor's labourer, until a factory inspector called his bluff and dismissed him as under age. It was a kind of literary debut. He found work in a bakery and a tiling factory and then, aged fourteen, enlisted in the King's Liverpool regiment. It was a choice between taking the shilling and starvation. The regiment counted as Irish and had been well infiltrated by Fenians; whenever there was trouble in Ireland its arms were placed under lock and key. They were ordered to Ireland when James was sixteen, and he saw for the first time, from the wrong end of a rifle, the country of his father John Connolly, who worked for the Edinburgh corporation first as a manure carter, then as a lamplighter and later as a lavatory attendant. Connolly deserted the army with four months' service still to go, a crime which went undetected as his records had been mislaid.

From then on he lived perpetually on the brink of starvation, working at various times as cobbler, pedlar, dustman, labourer, shipyard worker, dividing his time between those jobs and studying in public libraries. His squint came from reading at home in semi-darkness. He taught himself fluent

Gaelic, French, German and Italian, and later could address meetings of Italian workers in the US in their own language. In Edinburgh he organized for the Social Democratic Federation; on moving to Dublin he founded the Irish Socialist Republican party. He witnessed a famine in Kerry, and got involved with the starving peasantry. Then he emigrated to the US, worked with the Industrial Workers of the World and became national organizer of the Socialist Party of America. Back in Ireland the firebrand James Larkin was forming the Irish Transport and General Workers Union, fighting for the right of combination from town to town. Connolly returned to Ireland to find Larkin in gaol with hard labour on a trumped-up charge, fought for his release and joined him in organizing the transport workers. He led mill girls in a Belfast strike and foundry workers in Wexford, appeared on women's rights platforms throughout the nation and astonished cultivated London by effortlessly trouncing Hilaire Belloc in a debate at the London Irish Club. He met Eleanor Marx and was eagerly read by Lenin. In the great Dublin lock-out of 1913, with half the capital in revolt, he was thrown into prison and released after going on hunger strike. As the police rioted in Dublin, killing and maiming workers, he formed the Irish Citizen Army, later to become the nucleus of the Easter Rising. Drawing closer to the middle-class nationalists, he studied the tactics of street warfare and joined the inner councils of the Irish Republican Brotherhood. For twenty-six years he had organized tramway men, moulders, dockers, garment workers, milkmen and textile workers from Glasgow to Chicago, until a dumdum bullet on O'Connell Street had brought him to a final halt.

Connolly lay back on the sofa and watched images from the past flicker through his mind — Jim Larkin, smuggling himself into Dublin's Imperial Hotel to address the workers from its windows during the 1913 lock-out, fooling the police with a false beard and a cloak borrowed from Count Casimir Markievicz; the delighted cry of 'It's Larkin!' from the crowd below, as Jim thundered out a few words in his celebrated Ciceronian style before disappearing in a flurry of police fists; the fat Stetsoned strikebreakers of the Midwest armed with rifles and truncheons, who had chased him a mile through the streets of Chicago before beating him unconscious in a back alley; the aristocratic yobos of Oxford, breaking up one of his street meetings until in fury he seized the seven foot pole of the red flag from the platform, broke it over his knee and belaboured the offspring of the British ruling class all the way down St Giles. He had wandered later for two hours around Oxford in the dark, looking for a hat he had lost. None of it had come to much; he did not have much to show for those years. He had hated most of his time in the US, tossed between sectarian socialists who derided his religion and the power-hungry professional Irishmen who listened reverently to the words of a Roman pontiff at Sunday mass and spent the rest of the week campaigning against working-class Italians coming to live in their streets. Now he knew, he had remarked to a friend, where the snakes which St Patrick drove out of Ireland had taken up their residence.

In 1914 the working-class parties of Europe had cravenly thrown in their lot with imperialist war, Austrian socialists skewering the guts of their Russian comrades. Back in Ireland the socialists despised Connolly's republicanism as a bourgeois deviation, while the nationalists wished the holy cause of a united nation to be unsullied by class struggle. He had had some hopes for the Easter Rising, until the confusion of orders and loss of German arms made it inevitable that they would be defeated. As he lay wounded in bed in the post office he asked himself whether any political cause was worth the loss of Lillie and their five daughters, Nora, Aideen, Ina, Maire and Ruaidhre. Every bullet whining towards the post office spelt an absolute parting from them. And how much time had he spared them after all, for all his fine talk of women's rights and the sacredness of the family, dashing as he had done from Salford to Salt Lake City, studying Gaelic grammar and the small print of a boss's contract, selling newspapers on windy street corners, drilling his Citizen Army, mugging up Marxist economics and the ancient clan system of Ireland? Now he was likely to die as he had lived, fighting an enemy whose rhetoric he could counter without strain but whose violence seemed inexhaustible. Now he had run west, down his last cul-de-sac, and was doomed to spend his last days on earth with a monk and a clown.

He was uneasy about Molloy. Molloy was beginning to suspect, to see the truth about him. He had disowned it so far in his mind, but if they were holed up here together for much longer it would seep out in a stray gesture or unwary word. They were putting on a good act in front of the foreigners, but Molloy was compatriot enough to sense his deathliness. He would begin to infect him too before long, as he had done the others. Molloy was a zealous republican, loving his country fiercely, tenderly, like a bride; he himself believed absolutely nothing. It was too late for belief; all that was left was the rhetoric of it, like the fading after-image of a landscape he had once inhabited. The words were true enough as far as they went, but he had long since lost grip on whatever it was they corresponded to. He twiddled and turned them like knobs on a machine, not knowing whether they were still wired up, whether one cog was still meshing with another. He was operating the revolution like a pilot flying blind, entirely reliant on his rhetorical instruments. He had heard himself instructing the foreigners about the ten commandments, martyrdom, mythology, and felt like an actor performing a script in which he was word perfect but a script drafted in Swahili or

Serbo-Croat, as senseless as the cryptic script of the clouds. His pronunciation was impeccable but the words were dead letters, small shrivelled corpses littering the page. His whole political career seemed a long repetition of his first job as a child as a compositor's labourer, heaving around the heavy trays of type, setting the dull greasy blocks in rows which might somewhere enthral or outrage a reader but which for him was just mechanical labour. He had manipulated the words directly with his fingers, pressing them home into their trim ranks, as later he would reach through them to manipulate the admiring crowds, setting a hall alight with a well-slotted phrase, ranking his points on the back of an envelope for rhetorical effect. He could run his fingers over an audience, pressing his signs effectively into place, setting the machine of language in motion and watching its parts busily whirr. The parts meshed, articulated, engaged each other without slippage or excess, but he had long since lost all feel for what they represented. Maybe this was all the truth you could expect, this deft splicing of phrase with phrase, this small miracle of engineering as the machine hummed and throbbed with its own self-absorbed power.

Meanwhile he had let go, lapsing away into the silence of his own mind. He had begun addressing Lillie like a public meeting, and mild words for the children dried on his tongue. He had felt his foot explode on O'Connell Street in a scalding cascade of flame, and found himself a few seconds later lying with his nose squashed against the kerb, wondering impatiently how long an operation would take. His brain cleaved his body like a surgeon's scalpel, unscathed by the damage it wreaked, a flexed unblinking eye which nothing seemed to quench. It was a kind of madness, a queerness of the head. Others had begun to perceive that he was not quite right. They had begun to blight a little, their voices forced and faltering, in the shadow of death he cast over them. He wondered whether there was anything in him left to kill. Pieces of him had been flaking off for years, so that being shot seemed less some unspeakable rupture than logically continuous with what he was. He was merely waiting to go on stage to perform his dying perfunctorily in public. He had been up against the execution wall the whole of his life, and that knowledge had inscribed everything he had done like a ghostly trace, setting him free. It had given him the ironic detachment he had needed to come through, but now he was coming through to death empty-handed, more like a suicide than a martyr, without even an identity to be sacrificed or a body to be burnt. His detachment had become indifference.

He had no feeling for any of the men in the cottage, not even for Molloy. He would trade them all without compunction for a cause that was now no more than a piece of language. If salvation lay anywhere it lay in the word, but the word had to be its own reality. It was hopeless to ransack it any longer for hidden richness; it just was what it was. There was nothing behind it. It was not he that was behind his words, but that they were behind him. His whole life was a set speech, impersonal and pre-scripted, a paragraph from the penny catechism. The words would have to find their own way in the lives of others, breed their own feelings rather than draw upon his. He had told Wittgenstein that this would surely happen, that the Irish people would rise up, but he really had no clue. It was just the correct thing to say to a sceptical outsider. He had no idea any longer whether he even wanted the people to rise up. He despised the way they were so mindlessly enthused by his oratory, despised Molloy for his simple clodhopping faith. Molloy would make a good martyr because there was still blood in him. It was those like him who were fit to inherit a reborn Ireland; those like himself who had laboured all their lives to build it were the last people to be let loose there, spreading their deadly infection. He was impatient for death, as a final refuge from the tedium of contaminating others. He was the death rattle of an order about to topple, not a harbinger of the new. Ireland was a skeleton wearing a mask, a stately home scooped out and filled with a starving rabble. In that way alone was he its symbol.

Connolly opened his eyes in sudden panic, feeling a hand on his arm. Donal was standing over him with a dish of bacon, tendering it as reverently as if it were a communion plate.

Nine

A gunman was walking the road out from Galway. Dark-eyed, burly of build, not of Ireland. He passed the broken gate where Bakhtin had released the donkeys, swinging a battered bag at his side. He was following the winding track to Ballymeany, humming to himself soundlessly in his head. A thin quick stream ran by the road, and the gunman stopped and scooped up some of its water to drink. Then he sat down under a stone wall, fastened his bootlace and took a cheese sandwich from his bag. He leaned against the wall and watched a heron wheel and drop out of sight behind a shattered barn. The killer closed his bag, wiped his mouth with a palmful of stream water and walked on his way. He would be at the cottage by nightfall.

'Revolution,' Wittgenstein was telling Connolly, 'is the dream of the metaphysician.'

It was moonlit evening in Ballymeany. Connolly still lay on the sofa, with Wittgenstein sitting alertly across from him. Donal stumped in and out of the living room from time to time, ostensibly to dust, in fact to stare at his fellow countrymen. Bakhtin, itchy for air and exercise, lay on his bed, got up, paced around the house and lay down again. His body felt like a mummy's stale swaddling bands; he yearned to rip it down the middle and burst out of it with a roar. Molloy crouched by the window chain-smoking, still apparently awaiting reinforcements. It seemed to Bakhtin that time had been frozen by Connolly's entry into a vacant space where nothing flourished but repetition. They were like characters on a bare stage, waiting for a revolution which would never come. He marvelled, as he had often done in Cambridge, at Wittgenstein's extraordinary freshness. The man seemed inexhaustibly vigilant, insistently present like a high-pitched vibration on the air. Patches of dark sweat festooned the armpits of Bakhtin's shirt, and the air was acrid with Molloy's tobacco. Humped on the sofa, Connolly looked like a mound of abandoned rags surmounted by a clown's exaggerated pallor, shifting his foot continually to find ease. Only Wittgenstein sat upright like a bright parrot on its perch, his sleek head cocked inquisitively in Connolly's direction.

The Irishman considered the Austrian's statement with a puzzled air. 'I'm afraid you have the better of me there. I'm a soldier, not a philosopher. I don't grasp your meaning.'

'I mean that the idea of a total break in human life is an illusion. There's nothing *total* to be broken. As though all we know now could stop, and something entirely different start. That's absurd. How would we even begin to describe this new future, utterly different as it is from the present?'

'If total break is an illusion, so is pure continuity. In any case, such fantasies don't trouble me. I agree there can be no absolute transformation. One uses the materials to hand, booby-trapped as they are by the enemy's devices.'

Wittgenstein scented a kill. 'How can you use all this' — he swept his arm around the room — 'to create something new? It'd be like trying to use language to speak of what lies beyond it.'

'There are different languages. Some belong to the past, others point to the future.'

'Ah, that's certainly true. But language has its limits too.

The limits of language are the limits of our world. You've been running your head up against those barriers, trying to burst beyond them. That's why you've received' — he hesitated for a moment — 'certain bruises.'

'They are bruises well bought. What do you propose instead? That we should languish in the prison-house of language while our gaolers sport in their great houses?'

'I wouldn't wish you to misunderstand me,' said Wittgenstein. 'No doubt you think of me as a reactionary — the leftover of a dying bourgeoisie. That's so in one sense but not in another. I am no port-sodden English don to whom the very word bourgeoisie is offensive jargon. My home is in Vienna, a city which is no stranger to wars and revolutions. I'm also more Jewish than Gentile; I was spat on more than once at school. You see your people as slaves; my race is the most hounded in history. We have an affinity there, perhaps. I'm no defender of the British government, as my friend Bakhtin will tell you — a lot of fat old parasites who've never worked honestly in their lives. You've worked hard with your hands; they were one of the first things I noticed about you. So have I. I'm a philosopher, but I detest the trade, which is one reason why I'm here. It's ironic that I should flee to Ireland only to meet a fellow philosopher, for though you call yourself a soldier that's what you are. But you're more lethal than any of the old men I left behind. At least their ideas, if they can be graced with the title, don't take to the streets armed with machine guns, whereas your murderous abstractions dismember bodies. Don't think I lack sympathy with your passion; only a madman could approve of the world as it is. You think you have a lever to change all that at a stroke — a dream of totality beloved of the very thinkers you oppose. Who'll pay the price of this transformation? Not you but the people. Who are you to drive them through a cataclysm which might end up if you're lucky in a new way of doing economics? What difference does it make to those who milk the cows whose head is on the coins? And if in the process you deprive the people of what little they had before, if they can no longer even sit in the sunlight, then there's no torment in that Christian hell of yours too harsh for you. History is barbarism, to be sure. But I myself am terrified of pulling one thread of that web, for fear of what else I might unravel. Perhaps this is cowardice; perhaps I envy your certitude. But in the end I would rather have my cowardice than your certitude. It spears fewer bowels.'

'You speak as if we had a choice,' said Connolly. 'That's *your* fantasy — the academic habit of mind. There is no choice. Sooner or later those who are oppressed will rebel. It isn't up to us to decide.'

There was a sudden crash from the front porch, like the sound of falling iron. Molloy seized his revolver with a curse and glared out of the window towards the front door. The garden was dark, a little moonlit; he could see nothing. He strode to the door, listened through it for a moment, then released the lock slowly and threw the door abruptly open with his body sheltered behind it. His revolver poked out into empty space. He began to move forward gingerly onto the porch. 'Careful, lieutenant,' Connolly shouted from the sofa. 'Cover your left.' The sound had seemed to him to come from the left side of the cottage.

Molloy inched cautiously out into the night, his back to the open door. The two dustbins stood directly in front of him, just over an arm's length apart. One of them was swaying slightly, its lid upturned on the garden path. Molloy pointed his gun with both hands into the dustbin's gaping darkness.

'Come out of that,' he shouted harshly.

Nothing happened. Molloy swallowed hard and wondered whether to shoot into the bin. It might be a cat. Then a hand gripped the rim of the dustbin from the inside, fat and gold-ringed in the moonlight. After a moment a face poked out above the hand, olive-skinned, heavy-eyed, fleshy of jowl, faintly foreign.

'Good evening,' the intruder quavered bravely. Then he noticed Molloy's revolver and released a startled grunt.

'Come out of that,' Molly growled disgustedly.

Heaving a little to free his portly girth, Leopold Bloom stepped sheepishly out of the dustbin.

Molloy's forearm had Bloom pinned by the throat to the wall; Connolly held his revolver at the ready. Molloy wrenched Bloom's head violently back by the hair and asked: 'Is it the army you are?'

Bloom quivered and said nothing. Molloy reached back his hand and struck him with the back of it full force against his face. Blood trickled from the edge of Bloom's mouth. Wittgenstein leapt to his feet, his face savage with anger. 'Stop that!' he commanded Molloy. 'It's not you he's looking for!'

'Shut up,' Connolly growled to Wittgenstein, jerking his gun at him. 'If he's army he's got a bullet for us all. What's a slap in the face to that in God's name?'

'Is it the army you are?' Molloy hissed to Bloom again, twisting his arm up his back and bowing him to the floor. 'Is it a fucking Tommy you are?' he frisked Bloom's jacket with his free hand, spilling the contents of a wallet on the carpet. There were a few pound notes, a photograph of a woman, some grimy visiting cards. Molloy reached for a card and read *Leopold Bloom, Advertising Agent.*

'Advertising agent. So that's the tale, is it? And what in the name of God's a fucking advertising agent doing out here in the back of beyond?'

Bakhtin looked down on the kneeling Bloom and remarked absently: 'Another literary man.'

Wittgenstein's voice, high and imperious, rang out

suddenly. 'Leave him alone, I tell you! It's not you he's looking for.' He walked over to Bloom, pale-faced and panting, Molloy thrusting him off with one hand. 'You're from Cambridge, aren't you?' he asked the back of Bloom's neck, struggling to keep his voice even. 'You've come to search me out?'

'Fuck off, you,' Molloy muttered contemptuously.

Wittgenstein fell on his knees before Bloom, crouching low so as to peer upward into his face. 'Are you a pupil of Moore's?' he asked him in a whisper.

'Sit down,' Connolly barked at Wittgenstein, training his gun at his head. 'Get back in your chair you blithering idjit or by Christ I'll blast you back into it with this!'

Wittgenstein was on all fours in front of Bloom, his eyes gleaming. 'Answer me, man! Is it Russell or Moore? Haven't I seen you in King's?'

Bloom's shoulders began to heave a little up and down. Tears gathered in his eyes and fell from his heavy cheeks on to the carpet. Donal was hovering at the kitchen door, dancing from one foot to another in excitement. 'The dirty bollix!' he shouted at Bloom. 'The auld skite's a lousy spy, chief, can't you see it in his eyes? Shoot the auld knacker for Christ's sake,' he pleaded with Molloy. 'Won't it be turning us all over to the Tommies he'll be if you don't shoot the auld stumer where he's kneeling?'

Molloy placed his foot against Wittgenstein's shoulder and thrust him to the floor. Wittgenstein seized Molloy's foot in his mouth and began to bite his shoe like a mad dog. Molloy staggered backwards, one foot in Wittgenstein's mouth and one arm up Bloom's back. Donal ran for cover behind Bakhtin, who was studiously inspecting his stomach over by the window. 'Blast the old gobshite!' he screamed to Connolly. 'Blast the flaming lot of them for Jesus sake!'

Bloom's head sank downwards on his chest. A low wailing sound came from his mouth, and he fell forward stiffly onto his face. Molloy pulled his foot out of Wittgenstein's mouth, reached down and heaved Bloom onto his back. Bloom's face was waxen and bloodstained, his eyes shut.

'He's fainted,' observed Molloy briefly.

'Take him into the bedroom,' Connolly commanded. 'You,' he ordered Bakhtin, 'help the lieutenant carry him in.' Bakhtin and Molloy staggered with the plump body towards the bedrooms. Wittgenstein turned to stare at Connolly, his face gradually reverting to its usual colour. Connolly held his eyes and stared coolly back.

'And then I came back to Eccles Street and she was gone,' said Bloom gloomily. 'Packed all her things and left. There was a note on the table addressed to Poldy.'

'Poldy?' asked Bakhtin.

'Yes. That's her nickname for me. Leopold, you see.'

'That's strange. Poldy is the nickname of Ludwig's sister too. Leopoldine.'

'Oh,' said Bloom.

They were sitting in the kitchen drinking cocoa together. Bakhtin clucked soothingly and gave a compassionate shake of the head. 'She'd eloped with this young man — this student?'

'That's right. Stephen. She'd always fancied the educated type. Course I wasn't to know it'd get that far that soon. She'd only seen him once before, when I brought him back home after we'd been out on the town together. Then he got all depressed about Dublin and the street fighting, said it all showed Ireland was spiritually rotten and an old sow or something, and she was scared of the fighting and wanted to get out, so they took off to Paris together.' Bloom's fingers plucked glumly at the plaster on the side of his mouth. 'Said he was writing a book and he'd put her in it.'

Bakhtin nodded sagely. 'A familiar ploy. Put you in a

book, get you on stage, paint you in the nude.'

Bloom looked up sharply, a little startled by this last phrase. 'So I just came on out here. Couldn't work or sleep or anything. I just packed a bag and got away from it all.'

Bakhtin stared thoughtfully into his cocoa, then eyed Bloom with sudden tenderness. 'How are you feeling this morning? Your colour is much improved.'

'Oh, all right thanks,' replied Bloom, blushing faintly. 'I must have looked pretty silly, keeling over like that. Can't think what came over me. First time in my life I've fainted.'

Bakhtin looked at him wonderingly. Had he forgotten what had happened to make him faint? He peeped into Bloom's cloudless, bulging eyes and concluded he was a strange fellow.

'Course I'm not surprised Mr Molloy got a bit panicky,' Bloom went on charitably. 'Must have given him a bit of a turn, finding me in the dustbin. I felt a bit of a fool I can tell you. I was just wandering around the village and found this place and thought I'd sleep in the bushes, but it got a bit cold so I thought I'd try the dustbin, seeing as how it's a big one. Bit of a tight squeeze but I might have nodded off if Mr Molloy hadn't come out. And then when he brought me in and I saw James Connolly lying on the sofa I thought I'd gone to sleep in the bin and was dreaming. Phew!' Bloom whistled humorously and gave a rueful grin. 'Molly would have had a fit, I can tell you. She was always going on about how he'd be the ruin of the country and how she couldn't believe his moustache was real, she said it was one of those false ones he wore just to make himself look more important like.'

'You're not a republican yourself?'

Bloom hesitated a little. 'Well the thing is you see I'm not really Irish actually, I'm Hungarian, well my father was. So all this talk about Home Rule and the rest of it tends to pass me by a bit. Not that I'm against it or anything but I don't see why they have to go around shooting each other. Live and let live, that's my motto.'

'An excellent one,' said Bakhtin. He touched Bloom gently on the shoulder. 'Would you like to rest now? You must still be tired after your wanderings.'

'Oh no,' said Bloom brightly. 'Actually I'm quite looking forward to having a bit of conversation with Mr Connolly. Chance of a lifetime, really. I don't get much opportunity for intellectual conversation back home.' A thought shadowed his eyes. 'That's what I was hoping to get out of Stephen,' he added sadly.

'But instead,' observed Bakhtin gravely, 'he got something out of you?'

Bloom stared at his knees and said nothing.

'My friend,' said Bakhtin, 'do you know about women?'

Bloom looked up, perplexed. 'Women? Which women?' he thought.

'I mean the enigma of women.' Bakhtin took one of Bloom's hands delicately between his own. 'There is an old Russian folk tale; it concerns a young prince who had to choose between three caskets in order to win his bride. The first casket contained a single lily, wrapped round with a lock of the girl's hair. In the second lay the corpse of a newborn chicken with a sprig of myrtle in its mouth. The third casket held nothing but a toadstool and a mouldy piece of cheese.' Bakhtin squeezed Bloom's hand slowly and asked: 'You understand? You see what one must choose?'

Bloom looked at his hand in the Russian's hairy grip, then shyly up at his face. 'Yes,' he lied. 'I understand.'

Bakhtin rose, deposited his cocoa cup in the sink with a dramatic flourish, and turned dashingly on his heel at the door. 'Remember,' he said to Bloom. 'A lily, a chicken and a toadstool with a piece of cheese.' Then he winked broadly and padded off into the living room. Bloom sat on at the table, repeating Bakhtin's words carefully to himself. He had no idea what they meant, and neither no doubt did Bakhtin.

The kitchen door opened again to reveal Wittgenstein. He advanced slowly towards Bloom, one finger raised in admonishment. Then he stretched out the palms of his hand under Bloom's nose.

'Look at them. What do you see? Empty. Nothing.'

'Eh?' said Bloom.

'Empty as *this*.' Wittgenstein jabbed a finger to his forehead. 'Cleaned out. Finished. Philosophy is mad. Return to your Fenland masters and tell them what I've told you. Do you understand?'

'Yes,' Bloom lied again.

'There's nothing here for you. I can't stop writing, but it's all burnt. Every scrap.' He leaned across to Bloom, his lips an inch from his ear. 'Give it up!' he hissed. 'For God's sake give it up before we all go insane.'

Bloom pondered this for a moment. 'Right-ho,' he agreed.

Wittgenstein turned towards the door. 'About that of which we cannot speak ...' he murmured. He nodded slowly at Bloom. Bloom nodded slowly back.

Wittgenstein returned to the living room, leaving Bloom sunk in thought at the table. Can't stop writing, he says. That's a queer one. Could always try wearing boxing gloves. Get someone to tie them on, lots of knots, can't get one off with the other. Or a tablet maybe, some kind of contrascriptive. Dry up your ink. Or treat the paper chemically so the ink doesn't take, fades as you write, write all you want and damn all to show for it.

He was finding all of this extremely interesting. It was the first time in his life that anything had really happened to him, before Molly's elopement. He couldn't really blame her for that. He knew he was boring. If he had been her he would have gone off with Stephen too. The trouble was he always seemed to see the other man's point of view. Everybody else's views always struck him as better than his. Not that he had many views in the first place. Dublin was the most opinionated city on earth, everyone jumping down everyone else's throat, the public bars noisy with belief. It seemed to him all right as long as you didn't take it too far. Somebody always ended up having to put the cat out. If only he could get a bit worked up about something. He hadn't felt angry at all when Molly left him; he had cried and felt sick but there was none of the rage you read about in books. The trouble was that he wasn't really anything in particular. He wasn't a vegetarian or Plymouth Brother or anarcho-syndicalist. He was a Jew, but that wasn't the kind of thing you went around advertising. Better to keep your head down and merge with the crowd. Anyway, being a Jew was more something that happened to you than something you did. Sometimes he had this strange feeling he wasn't really there, as though he had spent all his life rather than just ten minutes hiding in a dustbin. He couldn't see why everybody had to be so opinionated. There was surely a little bit of truth in everything, well maybe not everything, but in most things. People said stupid things but they made sense to them, and you had to respect that. It would be a funny world if we all thought the same. He was going to pop next door in a minute and listen to Connolly but it was silly really because he would only end up agreeing with everything he said, which couldn't be right because not many people did. Still, one day he might do something. Nothing heroic, of course, just something to make a bit of a mark. Something to demonstrate that he really existed. He slipped into the living room, determined to disagree with everything he heard.

Ten

Donal piling sods of turf in the woodshed, thinking his own thoughts:

Yes and up each other's bums every night I'll be bound two old donkey-shaggers for all their fine talk revolution this and kiss me arse the other oh can't I see them now gobbling and sucking a treat and that little one with the funny eyes bent as a frigging horseshoe with his oh protect me they're after me have your cock out before look at you and the big bastard with the conk some kind of Russian is it Jew boy could be you don't need eyes in your head to see that boyo's liver's on the fucking blink like my da give him a couple of years and the little one with his burn it burn it I'm not as daft as I look I can come the old Irish as well as any of them if that mickey-dazzler really is your fine professor there's them over the water will pay good money for it and that scut with his post office post office! they couldn't knock off a fucking sweet shop up the republic and we ourselves and he not even born in the country foreign scum the lot spies and traitors but there's them in town will give me more than the price of a pint and then me boyos it's Holyhead for me.

'The same old tune,' Bakhtin was saying in the living room. 'A tale told by an idiot. History doesn't exist. *This*' — he smacked his belly — 'is what history can't encompass.'

'You don't establish a criterion of reality,' said Wittgenstein coldly, 'by an emphatic stress on the word "this". Or by punching your stomach, which in your case nothing could encompass.'

'Only philistines and politicians deny history,' said Connolly. 'If the ruling class admits that it was once born, then it also acknowledges that it can die.'

'Some nations,' remarked Bakhtin, 'die of inertia. The Irish will die of nostalgia.'

'The Irish need to keep remembering their past because the British keep forgetting it.'

'It seems to me,' said Bakhtin, 'that this uprising of yours is simply re-enacting the tragedy of the past. Only this time as farce.'

'If we republicans don't remember the past, who will? Our rulers rewrite it in order to make it continuous with the present. That's why not even the dead are safe from them.'

'Let the dead bury their dead,' said Bakhtin. 'It's through the past that death came into the world. The past reminds us that life is short, that the future will soon be over. That's why we claw so desperately at each other in the present. If we could only forget the past we might be free.'

'The past of this nation,' said Connolly, 'is certainly one the British would rather forget. They teach children in British schools about Good Queen Bess, but do they tell them that she mustered the greatest army of her reign to exterminate the Irish people? The poet Edmund Spenser, himself no friend of this nation, wrote of the defeated rebels crawling on their knees from every corner of the woods, happy to feed off dead carrion which they scraped from the graves, flocking to a plot of shamrock or watercress as to a sumptuous feast. Or perhaps the children are told of the time of Cromwell, who ordered that no quarter should be given to the garrisons of Wexford and Drogheda, who depopulated whole counties and drove Catholics from their land to the barren wastes of Connacht. Our people were forced down into destitution, barred from the vote and public office, and the price of five pounds on a priest's head was the same as that for a wolf. Swift wrote in bitter jest of our countryfolk eating their own children, but this was no idle fantasy for a race starved worse than the feudal vassals of Germany and Poland, screwed and wracked for their rents, a dozen of a family crammed into one miserable hovel with a single bed of straw, and the name of the Irish a byword throughout Europe for penury and wretchedness. I speak of British subjects, who when crushed in the repression of 1793 were hanged and had their bowels taken from their bodies while still alive and burnt before their eyes. Others were crucified, and crowned with linen caps full of burning pitch. But what was this to the million men, women and children who died in the great hunger, when ships from Europe bearing food for famine relief were amazed to meet six times their own number of merchant vessels bearing grain and cattle from Irish ports to Britain that could have fed our people twice over? Death and emigration reduced the Irish people by one third in those years, and during the reign of Victoria there were more evicted peasants than the entire population of Switzerland. Today cattle graze on tenantless farms, and the workhouses are crammed with paupers; the mortality rate of Dublin is higher than that of any other city in Europe. The British have reduced our history to a shambles, stolen our land, starved and slaughtered our people, gagged our tongues. Why then do they cry out in self-righteous fury when we strike against them?'

They sat in silence for a while. Bloom had been listening respectfully, chin in hands and elbows on knees. He liked a good story.

'Magnificent,' proclaimed Bakhtin. 'A breathtaking

performance. I congratulate you, sir. Not a word out of place. A brilliant narrative, though of course there's always another.'

'I'd fucking well like to hear it,' growled Molloy. He was faintly pale, moved by Connolly's words. He did not expect to live much longer, and was glad of such a vigorous reminder of what he was dying for.

'They drive us to despair,' Connolly went on, 'then brand us as savages when we strike back, blind to the mark of Cain on their own foreheads. Perhaps because we are an offshore island, speaking the language of the English because they thrust it down our throats, they can't see that they appear in our eyes as much an alien invader as ever the settlers of the West appeared to the Red Indians. If we Irish had occupied Kent and Sussex and Surrey, dispossessing the natives of their land, robbing them of their civil rights, forcing their children to learn Gaelic in school, inflicting savage penalties upon them for practising their Protestant religion, would the English have accepted this lightly? And would they have ceased to struggle against us just because all this was ancient history? The British will abandon India and Africa and the West Indies before they relinquish their grip on us, because it's clear even to them that such peoples perceive them as unwelcome strangers. Perhaps our skins should have been black; then the British might have begun to recognize what they were dealing with. Why can't they leave us in peace? What else have we been to them over these centuries but a burden and an embarrassment? Wouldn't they be happy to turn their backs on this impossible island, in which they see their own reflection monstrously distorted? It's their greed, not our need to be civilized, which bolts them to us. And even if the present struggle succeeds, if we wrest some independence from the Crown, the British will fight tooth and nail before they let go of the northern counties whose industry profits them most. They've skilfully prepared against this by fostering divisions between Catholic and Protestant, dividing the people to secure their rule. But if they insist on retaining that choice morsel in the north, they will be sowing a whirlwind and will reap the bitter fruits of it in the future. They won't understand this because in their hearts they take nothing that happens in this country seriously. I was told in the post office that when the British prime minister heard of our insurrection he said "well, that's really something," and went to bed. The British don't believe Ireland is real; they just dump their fantasies here.'

'You tell a grim tale,' said Wittgenstein, 'but it leaves us all impotent. How is this revolution of yours to raise the dead?'

'The dead can't be raised. They can simply be given a different meaning by what we do in the present. That's a kind of redemption.'

'That's bollock,' declared Wittgenstein firmly. 'Meaning isn't just something you decide on, like a different colour of wallpaper.'

'Personally,' said Bakhtin, 'I don't mind what meaning I have as long as I'm not dead.'

'You tell your story,' Wittgenstein said, 'to stir your people to revolt. Don't you see it will have precisely the opposite effect? How could anybody hope to escape from all *that*? The thicker you paint the horror, the more you paralyze hope.'

'At the centre of my religion,' said Connolly, 'is a broken body. It's there to scandalize the idealists of this world — those who seek comfort in the thought that human societies aren't so bad after all. That body states that if we fight for justice we'll be done to death by the state. Perhaps it's impossible to look on that body and live. I don't believe so.'

'I have looked on that body,' said Wittgenstein. 'It's all there is.'

'The dead can't be raised,' said Bakhtin, 'because they don't exist. Tragedy is a ruling-class conspiracy.'

'The future doesn't exist either,' replied Connolly. 'The British have deprived us of many things, but they've been foolish enough to leave us our dead, and that will be their undoing. The grass grows sooner over a battlefield than over a scaffold. To be free you to have to remember. It's not dreams of liberated grandchildren which spur men and women to revolt, but memories of enslaved ancestors.'

'I wish your revolt well, my friend,' said Bakhtin, 'but beware that you don't end up merely repeating the same old story. The state abhors only one thing in the end, and that's the sound of laughter. Violence it can understand. Only those who mock power are truly free of it; you are seeking power, and so will always be oppressed by it. I don't hear much laughter in this revolution of yours; it strikes me as just as poker-faced as what went before. Your socialism is just the dreary old Enlightenment in wolf's clothing, that deadly dream of Reason which has already chilled most of Europe to the bone. Now you propose to bring it to Ireland. You're like the Bolsheviks in my own country: all they can think of pitting against the Kremlin is efficiency and electrification. Look at Lenin: the Tsar with a megaphone. If they win they'll terrorize the nation with their demented Reason, they'll enlighten the peasantry to a pile of bones. The Bolsheviks have no bodies, they know nothing of pleasure and so are the sworn enemies of the people. The people want carnival, not collective farms; they know the only lasting revolution is one of the flesh. Answer the British with ridicule, my friend, not with rifles. Ride their dimwitted monarch backwards on a donkey with a stick of rhubarb up his fat bum. There are too many tight-lipped dashing young heroes in this uprising of yours. All small nations are obsessed with their virility: you hate the British so much because you fear that your willies have wilted. They've castrated you in the cradle, and you're seeking to redeem your shamed manhood in the eyes of your womenfolk. Where are these womenfolk, may I ask? There seems a curious absence of them in these environs. Three male philosophers sitting around talking politics: it's a familiar image of how the world is changed, or not as the case may be. I fear for your revolution, my dear sir; I fear it will never succeed because you've not yet learnt to be frivolous.'

'And while you lot are splitting your old ribs,' said Molloy, 'our lot are having them broken by the British army. Do you find that amusing now?'

'There's a tradition of humour in Ireland,' said Bakhtin. 'It's a precious revolutionary weapon.'

'There is,' said Molloy. 'Gallows humour.'

'There's also a tradition of poetry. Where's the poetry of this insurrection?'

'The chief's a poet,' said Molloy.

'Not a good one,' interposed Connolly. 'But it's true that I've published verse.' He looked across at Bakhtin. 'I understand your meaning better than you think. Pleasure and humour are what we're fighting for. But while the fighting goes on I'm afraid they're expensive luxuries.'

'In that case you might just as well give up. You're using obsolete weapons — just as you do in your reactionary passion for equality, another grey yardstick of the bourgeoisie. There's no equality, only difference. Split that difference and you'll find more difference, and so on down to the tiniest atom through whose space you might just manage to heave your buttocks to see innumerable angels dancing on a pinhead.'

'I'm not sure,' said Connolly slowly, 'whether that's said seriously or in jest.'

'So much the worse for your revolution,' replied Bakhtin, stifling a yawn. He glanced at Bloom, who was sitting bright-eyed, upright, mouth slightly open, like a schoolboy laboriously following a lesson. 'Mr Bloom, we are eager to hear your voice. Are you revolutionary, reactionary, Christian, Mohammedan, all of these things together or nothing whatsoever?'

'I'm Jewish,' said Bloom, flushing faintly. Wittgenstein looked at him with sudden interest. 'Mind you, it's not easy being Jewish in this country, I can tell you. There aren't many of us around. Still, it takes all kinds as they say.'

'What takes all kinds?' asked Wittgenstein peevishly.

'You know: it takes all kinds to make a world.'

Wittgenstein stared at him with outraged eyes. 'That,' he murmured, 'is a very beautiful and very kindly saying. "It takes all kinds to make a world." I must remember that.'

'I don't mean I'm against revolution,' Bloom went on, emboldened by Wittgenstein's approval. 'It's just the violence I can't sort of adjust to. If we could have a revolution and put things to rights without killing anybody I'd be in there like a shot.'

'Mr Bloom,' said Bakhtin to Connolly, 'is a citizen of your country, though he isn't Irish by birth. Does your great movement include him too, or is it a matter of Ireland for the Irish?'

'We're not a sectarian movement. I myself was born in Scotland.'

'Then I fail to understand your obsession with national identity,' said Bakhtin. 'What's so glorious about this nationhood of yours? Or about identity for that matter? What is Nikolai Bakhtin? A minor tangle in the web of history, a random convergence of forces. It's just the same with nations.'

'It's not a question of asserting our identity, but of discovering one. We need to be free to find out what we might become. At present it's impossible for us to say who we are.'

'It's always impossible to say who one is. That's to be

celebrated, not regretted.'

Molloy looked over his shoulder and said: 'We're all Irish in the eyes of God.'

'Nationalism,' said Connolly, 'is like class. You have to have it in order to be rid of it. It's not an end in itself. Our movement draws its strength from national traditions, but this isn't a matter of banshees and leprechauns. We can leave all that to Mr Yeats and his crew, whose souls are half-British anyway. We've always looked to Europe for our ideas, from the time of Duns Scotus to the days of Wolfe Tone. An Irishman who throws a stone at a foreigner risks hitting one of his own clansmen.'

'So you might even learn from the British?' asked Bakhtin mischievously.

'Oh indeed. We look with respect on their great national literature: Swift and Sterne, Goldsmith and Burke, those twin giants of the London stage Wilde and Shaw. A pity we can produce nothing to compare to them.'

'Your writers seem curiously eager to desert your shores.'

'Indeed. As they say, the quickest way to Tara is the boat to Holyhead. What was there for them here? The British reduce us to a famished land whose bleakness drives out our poets, then boast of having stolen our writers. If the Irish are an international race, we have the British to thank for it.'

'You're certainly less parochial than the British,' Bakhtin agreed, 'though that's hardly difficult. There are no ideas in England, only customs.'

'All nations which subjugate the world condemn themselves to insularity. They believe themselves superior, and detest ideas because they might tell them otherwise. The most inbred nation is the one with its gunboats in every continent.'

'No danger of inbreeding here,' said Bakhtin. 'A Scottish Irishman, an Irish Hungarian, an anglicized Austrian and a

Russian. Not a decent Englishman among us.'

'But you'll notice that we all use their tongue. The English learn their language in the cradle; I had to wait until I had children of my own. No wonder they have us by the throat.'

'There's no such thing as a native language,' said Bakhtin dismissively. 'All languages are strange, and none is. I speak seven of them, of which Russian happens to be the one I acquired first. Some hanker for Eden; personally I've always preferred Babel.'

'I speak more than one language too. But you share the privilege of those whose tongues were not locked up in their heads by Act of Parliament.'

Molloy interposed: '*Éiríonn teanga duine éigin dúchasach nair a goideann duine eile é.*'

'He says,' translated Connolly, 'that one's language becomes native when it is stolen by somebody else.'

Wittgenstein spoke up suddenly in his high voice, startling Bloom a little. 'You speak of languages as though they were garments to be put on and off at will. There are limits to such cosmopolitanism. In the end, we speak as we do because of *what* we do. *Wenn ein Löwe sprechen könnte, würden wir ihn nicht verstehen*'. [If a lion could speak, we would not be able to understand him.]

Bakhtin gave a roar of laughter. '*Togda ty sam, dolzhno byt, lev, Lyudig,*' he said, '*tak kak nikto ne ponimaet chto ty govorish.* A little joke,' he added modestly. 'I said in that case Ludwig must be a lion, since nobody can understand what he says.'

Bloom licked his lips, glanced nervously around the company and said: '*az embert a nyelv teszi nagyobbá az allatoknál. Ez a tragediája.* An old Hungarian proverb,' he explained shyly. 'Language is what makes man greater than the beasts. That is his tragedy.'

'A gem,' murmured Bakhtin, treating Bloom to a soft clapping of the palms. 'Exquisitely phrased and profoundly true.'

'No, it isn't,' said Bloom. He had decided to be argumentative. 'You're only saying that because it's foreign. You wouldn't say that if I'd said "In for a penny, in for a pound" or something.' Well, in for a pound, he thought. 'I don't think this conversation's getting anywhere. It's just a lot of abstract ideas.'

'Agreed,' said Wittgenstein. 'Any pig can have ideas.'

'Why don't we talk about real people for a change?' asked Bloom.

'Ideas are what real people are made of,' said Bakhtin. 'What they live by.' He glanced across at Connolly. 'Or die by.'

'That's stupid,' said Bloom. 'I don't live by ideas and I wouldn't die for one either. That's not what matters.'

'What do you think matters?' asked Bakhtin.

'Love,' said Bloom. 'I mean the opposite of hate.'

'That's an idea,' said Bakhtin.

'It's strange to think of love and hate as opposites,' said Connolly. 'They seem to me inseparable.'

'That's just abstract too,' said Bloom. 'We just sit here spouting theories. Why don't we try to get to know each other instead? We don't seem like real people here, just stereotypes — stereotypes talking a lot of hot air. Doesn't anyone here have a private life?'

'Privacy,' said Wittgenstein, 'is a philosophical error.'

'Why don't we *do* something?' asked Bloom. 'Why don't we just get up and go?'

'We can't,' said Molloy. 'We're waiting for reinforcements.'

'Talking is a form of doing,' said Wittgenstein.

'Crap,' said Bloom.

'We could all go for a drink,' suggested Bakhtin, 'or one of us could say something in his own language and the rest of us could try to guess what it meant.'

'That's stupid,' said Bloom. 'Silly games. Anyway, that

was all the Hungarian I know. Maybe we should sit round calling each other names.'

'I thought that's what we were doing,' said Bakhtin.

'Or we could tell each the other something important about ourselves. Something that nobody else knows.'

'Nothing is concealed,' said Wittgenstein. 'Everything that's important lies open to view.'

'Tell that to my wife,' said Bloom. They sat around in silence for a moment. 'I mean, we've got Mr Connolly here, who's supposed to be one of the greatest men in the country, and what do we do? Just talk a lot of tripe. Nobody bothers to find out what kind of a person he is. We haven't even asked him if his leg's hurting.'

'James Connolly,' said Bakhtin, 'is a stereotype — a symbol. That's what so fascinating about him. Individuals you can meet any day; you don't often run into a symbol.'

'I'm not bothered about his politics,' said Bloom. 'You can stuff politics. I'm interested in him as a person. I'm interested in all of you as people.'

'I used to be a person,' said Connolly, 'I'm not sure I am now. It's a little late for that.'

'What's this revolution of yours about then if it's not about people,' said Bloom. 'Donkeys?'

'Those of us who make the revolution may not be the best image of the lives we hope to make possible. We have to harden ourselves to misery in order to end it.'

'I suppose,' said Wittgenstein, 'that that's what Marxists call dialectical and the rest of us call devious.'

'When the people have withered away,' intoned Bakhtin, 'the state will enter upon a new freedom.'

'The only problem,' Bloom said to Connolly, 'is that you're the people making the future and we're the people who are going to have to live in it. Those of us still on our feet when you've stopped shooting, that is. How are symbols going to create real people?'

'I admire your concern for the individual,' said Bakhtin. 'It's very stereotypical.'

'Oh, I'm a stereotype alright. I'm foreign, I'm Jewish, my wife has just run off and left me. Nothing special; millions like me. But I'm still *me*, aren't I?'

'There is no more useless proposition,' said Wittgenstein, 'than a thing's identity with itself.'

'Bollocks,' said Bloom. 'You can't feel my pain. None of you can feel my pain.'

'Sensations,' said Wittgenstein, 'don't belong to individual bodies like private property. That's a philosophical error.'

'Bullshit,' said Bloom. 'I don't give a fart in my corduroys about philosophy. Philosophy's just a fancy name for not caring about people. All this talk about raising the dead. You couldn't even raise an eyebrow. Just a lot of empty words. What do you really care about?' he asked Wittgenstein.

'Forms of life,' said Wittgenstein.

'Arseholes,' said Bloom.

'The individual is supremely valuable,' said Bakhtin. 'A supreme fiction, too. But what of that?'

'You might be a bleeding fiction,' said Bloom. 'You look pretty much like one to me. I happen to be real. I think I'm just about the only real person here. The only reason you lot talk about the dead so much is because you're all dead yourselves. Just a bunch of zombies talking about talking. Why don't we do something?'

'We are doing something,' said Wittgenstein.

'Call this living?' said Bloom. 'I'd rather be dead.' They sat around in silence. 'Well, what should we talk about now? I reckon we're just about cleaned out, don't you? Anyone got any jokes? We could all tell a joke in our own language and the rest of us could sit around not laughing. You got any good Gaelic jokes?' he asked Molloy. Molloy was silent. 'I think you *are* a good Gaelic joke.'

'What was that you said?' asked Molloy.

'Forget it. I'm just a fiction, remember? Everything's just a fiction.'

'You watch your mouth,' said Molloy, 'or you might find yourself under six feet of good Gaelic earth.'

'That'd be doing something, wouldn't it?' said Bloom. 'Or would it just be language or something?'

'I have a suggestion,' said Bakhtin pacifically, turning to Connolly. 'Our nerves are becoming a little frayed here. Would it be permissible for one of us to take some exercise? Myself, preferably.' His body felt rusty with disuse. 'I assure you I'll speak to no one.'

Connolly and Molloy eyed each other uncertainly. 'Very well,' said Connolly, 'but the lieutenant must accompany you. You can go out by the back door and take the path up to the cliff, but not too far.' He looked across to Molloy. 'Stand where you can keep an eye on him and the cottage too.'

Bakhtin bowed deeply, put on his cloak and disappeared with Molloy into the kitchen. Bloom sat glowering hotly at his knees. Wittgenstein eyed Connolly warily and said: 'You were speaking of a cosmopolitan revolution. That's a contradiction in terms.'

'I don't follow you.'

'There are various language games, as I've called them in my work; all tangled, crisscrossed, overlapping to infinity. You think you've found a tongue which underlies them all. One might call it the language of the body — of death, martyrdom and resurrection. A pure speech into which all others can be translated.'

'I don't know. Maybe that's what I believe.'

'Your death won't act as a dictionary to unlock these other tongues. It won't unravel the web of injustice; it'll merely contribute another strand to it.'

'Whether you're right or not is irrelevant. I can't turn back now, even if I wished. Would you have me do?'

'Stop trying to walk on pure ice. Return to the rough ground while there's still time.'

'You see me as a purist,' said Connolly. 'That's ironic: it's just how I see you. You look at me and see your own guilty desire. That's why you're so afraid of me; if I was simply an enemy you wouldn't be so uneasy. You feel easy with your Russian friend because he's everything you're not. I told you that crisis in this country is commonplace. I'm no absolutist.'

'You're absolute for death — as though it were an extreme limit on which to stand. There's no such place.'

'It's you who urge tolerance and can't bear to be crossed.'

'Perhaps I don't know how to speak to a man in the presence of death,' said Wittgenstein. 'About that of which we cannot speak, we must remain silent.'

'We're always in the presence of death,' said Connolly. He raised himself a little on the sofa, as if reminded of something. 'Where's your man?' he asked harshly.

Eleven

Bakhtin was lying on the cliffs, the sound of the ocean in his ears, dreaming of Tanya. She stood over him, naked except for her embroidered headband. He could see the soft upward tilt of her breasts and the downy dark hair of her belly. He opened his mouth in surprise but Tanya shook her head quickly and placed a roguish finger to her lips. She crouched down, straddling him with her knees and pressing her thighs to his sides. Then she leant forward, plump breasts dangling over him, and placed her lips on his.

There was something wrong with Tanya's mouth. Instead of the moist warmth he remembered, Bakhtin encountered something hard, bitter-tasting, metallic. Tanya was mocking him, forcing his lips apart with her tongue but jeeringly, cynically, not with the playful tenderness he knew. He opened his eyes in alarm to find the muzzle of a rifle inserted into his open mouth. A soldier stood holding the weapon, his face distorted by sunlight. Other soldiers in khaki stood around, staring down silently.

'Sweet dreams, squire?' said the man holding the rifle. 'We've been well away, haven't we, Mr Connolly? Try to move and I'll blow your fucking head off.'

Bakhtin closed his eyes again and let his head sink back on the grass, trying vainly to resummon Tanya.

Connolly had heard the soldiers drive up and crawled off his sofa, dragging his crutches behind him. He managed to get himself out of the back door and made off on hands and knees up the cliff path, searching for a rock to hide behind. Bloom had run out frantically into the garden, diving behind a clump of bushes just in time to avoid being spotted. The men who had arrested Bakhtin marched him at gunpoint into the cottage as four or five others were holding down Wittgenstein on the kitchen table. Captain Jeremy Chapman bounded lankily in through the front door, pistol cocked, short fair hair flopping. The sergeant guarding Bakhtin saluted sloppily and said: 'We fink it's Connolly, sir.'

''E were lying on grass,' added his Lancashire companion, eager to announce his presence at the crucial scene.

Chapman saw a man one and a half time's Connolly's size. He pressed his revolver to the soft flesh above Bakhtin's beard and said: 'Are you James Connolly?' He wanted to hear his accent.

Am I James Connolly? thought Bakhtin. Perhaps. Why not? 'Indeed, my dear sir,' he boomed, 'I am James Connolly.'

Chapman raised his gun lightly and crashed it against the Russian's right temple. Blood spurted from Bakhtin's scalp and welled darkly over his eyes. 'And I'm Herbert Asquith,' said Chapman good-humouredly. He yanked roughly at Bakhtin's beard with his free hand. 'You think Connolly had time to grow this?' he asked the sergeant. 'Are you searching out back?' The sergeant nodded. An acned young private put his head around the kitchen door. 'There's a German or something here, sir,' he called excitedly. 'We think it might be Sir Casement.'

'Bring him out,' ordered Chapman. Roger Casement, he knew, was in league with the Germans, not one of them, and already in custody. This should be pointed out to the private later for his military education.

They brought Wittgenstein in from the kitchen, bent double as though someone had been dancing on his stomach. There were cuts on his forehead, the other side from Bakhtin's. Suspended like a puppet between two soldiers, he cranked himself painfully upright. Chapman lowered his gun in astonishment.

'Professor Wittgenstein!' he exclaimed. He had read philosophy at Cambridge a few years previously, and had attended a few of Wittgenstein's lectures in Trinity.

Wittgenstein's glazed eyes fastened on the officer until his features swam into focus: flaxen hair, full fleshy lips, pale freckled skin, no chin to speak of. A dim memory stirred in his head.

So I was right, he told himself with grim satisfaction. This is where philosophy gets you.

Connolly was hiding behind a rock a few hundred yards from the cottage, revolver in hand. He could hear the soldiers scrambling up the path, their heavy boots scrunching fragments of stone. They were almost upon him. Not here, he told himself, heart leaping with fright. Better to be executed in Dublin than die like a dog in the middle of nowhere. He began to say the act of contrition, prudently choosing the shorter version. Jesus Mary and Joseph be with me in my hour of death. Better for the cause to die in Dublin. The cause? Don't fool yourself, it's fear. Better for the cause anyway, fear or not, to hell with it.

'You're all right now lads,' he called out, throwing his gun as high in the air as he could. 'You're fine now my boys. Not a drop of fight left in me. Easy does it now lads.' They crept cautiously around the rock, with orders to take him alive if possible, to find him lying on his back, grinning up to disarm them, his foot resting on a stone.

Bakhtin and Wittgenstein were placed in a car outside the cottage, to be driven off to Galway for interrogation. Bakhtin was mopping his head with a bloodied handkerchief. Chapman nodded genially to his old professor, to communicate that there would be no trouble for Cambridge men. Connolly was brought out of the front door on his crutches, covered by a rifle.

'Are you the owners of this cottage?' he asked the men in the car politely. 'I'm sorry if I've brought you trouble. I've been hiding out behind your house.'

'Not at all,' replied Wittgenstein with grave courtesy. 'You've brought no trouble to us. We wish you luck.'

Finbar Tierney came staggering around the corner from his bar, carrying a half-drunk bottle of whiskey. He stood for a moment swaying on his feet and staring at the soldiers, a vacant grin spreading beneath the busted nose. The Lancashire corporal swung his rifle at Finbar's head.

'Fuck off, Paddy. Fuck off, you turd.'

Finbar stared at Connolly, a flicker of recognition stirring somewhere in his skull. Then it fizzled out again as quickly as it came. He looked down at the corporal's rifle, grinned absently, and lurched off back around the corner, drinking as he went.

Connolly stared after Bakhtin and Wittgenstein as their car drove away. Chapman turned to his sergeant and said, 'Get everyone out over the cliffs. There could be more of them.' He did not believe this, but wanted to be left alone for a while with Connolly.

'Shouldn't some of us stay and guard him, sir?' the sergeant asked nervously. He knew what Chapman was like; it was the prisoner's life he feared for, not the officer's.

'Get them out on the cliffs,' snapped Chapman, 'and leave me a bayonet in case he makes trouble.'

The soldiers fanned out behind the cottage, uncertain what they were supposed to be doing, peering perfunctorily behind knee-high rocks until they disappeared in a straggling line over the crest of the cliff. Chapman raised the bayonet and dented the flesh of Connolly's neck with its tip, flicking it lightly from side to side. Connolly looked into his eyes, draining his face carefully of expression, and saw that he was serious. Prisoner injured while attempting to escape. Over Chapman's shoulder he could see Molloy squirming along on his stomach by the garden wall, revolver at the ready. He held Chapman's eyes steadily but he was looking at Molloy. Chapman was pressing the bayonet tip gradually harder against his neck. *Shoot him,* he urged Molloy in his mind. What are you waiting for? Kill him, you stupid bastard. *Shoot him in the back.* He watched an impulse flicker in Chapman's eyes: Molloy was ten yards away; had Chapman heard him? The bayonet hand drew back a fraction, ready to jab.

Molloy leapt noiselessly onto Chapman's back, wrenching him hard around the throat and fumbling for the bayonet. 'Use your gun!' Connolly barked, too late. Chapman, well-seasoned by Winchester and Sandhurst, staggered violently, kept his feet, twisted his bayonet arm awkwardly round and speared Molloy full in the stomach with a backward thrust. Molloy fell screaming to the ground, writhing and jerking with indecent abandon. His gun flew into the air and landed in the garden. Piercing shrieks tore open his mouth.

'Kill him properly,' Connolly said to Chapman. 'Kill him properly, you cunt.'

Chapman turned to his prisoner, white-faced and panting, then looked down at the threshing Molloy. 'Irish shithouse,' he said quietly. 'Fucking Fenian scum.' He glanced up at Connolly. 'Would you like to watch him die slowly? Or should I help him on a bit?' He reached down with the bayonet and ripped it once across Molloy's thigh, redoubling his screams. Leopold Bloom stepped out from behind the bushes, picked up Molloy's gun and shot Chapman in the back. Chapman sat down for a moment on his backside and then fell forwards and sideways, his arm twisted under his body. Molloy was still jerking and moaning. Bloom opened his eyes and saw what he had done. From a long way off he could hear Connolly's voice calling to him.

'Shoot him too,' Connolly was telling him. 'Bloom, shoot him too.'

Bloom staggered over to the garden wall and looked down at Molloy. A hot sick pressure gripped his chest, and he vomited violently over Molloy's boots. He gripped the revolver with both hands as he had seen Molloy do, and fired again. Molloy leapt once in the air, gurgled noisily and lay still.

'Throw the gun near his hand.' Connolly was saying. 'Bloom, throw the gun near his hand.'

Bloom threw the gun onto Molloy's dead body and ran back to the bushes, heaving as he went. Soldiers were running down the path behind the cottage and swarming over the cliff.

Twelve

'If he succeeds I am lost,' thought Wittgenstein. The car was bumping along the road back to Galway, cutting through great tracts of bog. He looked at the back of the driver's neck, its flesh rucked into pink rolls by the tight khaki collar. Another soldier was sitting between him and Bakhtin, seizing the chance of a cigarette. The Russian sagged heavily in his seat, face sick and grey, forehead hugely swollen. He had enjoyed the drama immensely, all but the final scene, and would dine out on it for the rest of his days. Wittgenstein tried to collect his thoughts but they were seized by the wind and whirled over the rocky fields. I am lost, he thought, I am back where I began. There is no common people, there is Connolly, Donal, Molloy. The more simple, the more complex: a barren life breeds fanaticism. What if philosophy and the people are not strangers? Connolly is a common man, yet a philosopher. A crank, maybe; but a crank is an instrument which makes revolutions. What if he is right that crisis is common? The people will deride this folly, live on in the innocent self-evidence of their gestures. There is no resurrecting the dead. If the dead rise I am done for. I thought I had touched rough ground, but there may be bog beneath. If he succeeds I shall have to start again. It will not be the first time.

The car dipped towards a hollow in the road where mist spilled from the fields, shrouding a humped bridge and the stream rushing beneath it. They moved forward into the mist and Wittgenstein looked across at Bakhtin to see him slowly blotting out, clotting up piece after piece with whiteness until he was no more than a frail suggestion on the air. The hood trapped the mist against cheekbone and eye socket, the body sagging beneath. The last act, Connolly thought to himself beneath the blindfold; God send I don't make a balls of it. The Fusiliers' breath steamed rawly in the drizzle, while McGrath ran back through the execution shed to fetch a rope. Nothing to be done but sit it out. Finish it off so we can get started. Invisible hands trussed him around the chest; he was about to go on. You must go on, I can't go on, I'll go on. See this bungled charade through to an end. He heard the officer call the squad to attention and felt the priest and warders withdraw from his side. As the rifles were raised he was already fading, dwindling, fragments of his body flaking away to leave only an image beneath. When the bullets reached him he would disappear entirely into myth, his body nothing but a piece of language, the first cry of the new republic.